EllRay Jakes
Stands Tall!

EllRay Jakes
Stands Tall!

BY **Sally Warner**

ILLUSTRATED BY
Brian Biggs

VIKING

VIKING

An imprint of Penguin Random House LLC
375 Hudson Street
New York, New York 10014

First published in the United States of America by Viking,
an imprint of Penguin Random House LLC, 2016

Text copyright © 2016 by Sally Warner
Illustrations copyright © 2016 by Brian Biggs

LIBRARY OF CONGRESS CATALOGING-IN-PUBLICATION DATA IS AVAILABLE
ISBN: 978-0-451-46913-7 (hardcover)
ISBN: 978-0-14-751253-6 (paperback)

Manufactured in China

1 3 5 7 9 10 8 6 4 2

Designed by Nancy Brennan   Set in ITC Century

To Liam and Fynn DiMaio —S.W.

• ◗ •

For Wilson and Elliot —B.B.

CONTENTS

* * *

EllRay Jakes
Stands Tall!

✳ **1** ✳

ALMOST LIKE B-BALL

"Give it here," I shout to Jared Matthews. He is hogging the basketball, as usual—not that he really knows how to play.

It is Tuesday afternoon recess on a cool-warm February day that is perfect for running around. Sunshine, wind, and freedom!

My name is EllRay Jakes, and I am eight years old. I am in Ms. Sanchez's third grade class at Oak Glen Primary School, in Oak Glen, California.

And I'm the shortest kid in class.

All I want is respect, but to get respect you have to be good at something. At home, with neighbor kids and friends, it could be video games and memorizing lists of anime names. But at school, it pretty much has to be sports. For us boys, anyway. And sports means doing stuff.

But running around is about all we're doing this

recess, because we don't really know how to play basketball—or "b-ball," as a couple of the guys in my class call it. Instead, we play something *almost like* b-ball.

Because with Jared, b-ball is more like a game of keep-away.

For Kevin McKinley and Nate Marshall, b-ball always ends up turning into soccer. They either bounce the ball off their heads, or they zig-zag kick it across the playground toward an imaginary goal. They make their own crowd-cheering sounds as they run.

When Kry Rodriguez gets hold of the ball, she stares at the hoop for so long before she shoots that some kids get bored and wander away. It's like Kry is doing yoga, something the girls in our third grade class are obsessed with lately.

Don't ask. I think yoga is mostly just holding still or lying around. In other words, it is the exact opposite of anything boy.

Jason Leffer just tucks the basketball under his arm like a football, ducks his head, and starts running.

Wrong game, dude!

My friend Corey Robinson is probably the best athlete in our whole school. He is a prize-winning swimmer. But he doesn't even try to get the ball. He's just glad to be outside, away from math, the white board, and reading out loud in class.

My new friend Marco Adair is the only other boy in class who is as bad at b-ball as I am. But Marco is too busy in his secret world of dragons and knights to care.

Me, I'd just like to get my hands on the ball for once! I can almost smell its weird rub-bery sweet-ness and feel its goose bumps under my fingertips.

Huh. I wish!

"Give it here," I yell again, darting around Nate and Major Donaldson, who are shoving each other in a friendly way that could turn rough, just like that.

"Come and get it, wuss," Jared shouts back, like he just won a prize. The prize for embarrassing me, I guess. He doesn't even care about breaking our school's no-name-calling rule.

"You guys are so lame," Cynthia Harbison shouts from over by the fence. "You don't even know what you're doing!"

"She's right," her personal assistant Fiona McNulty says. "I've seen real basketball on TV, you guys. With my *daddy*. And that's not it."

By now, we have three balls going at the same time, one basketball and two kickballs. So Fiona's at least a little right.

Jared tosses the real basketball up in the air, then spikes it down hard—volleyball style—in Cynthia and Fiona's direction.

Bam!

"Here! Throw it here," I shout to Fiona. But she is cringing against the chain link fence like she's still under attack.

"Cynthia," I yell. "Grab the ball and throw it here!"

"Get it yourself, if you want it so much, EllRay," Cynthia says, tossing back her hair and grabbing hold of Fiona's hand so they can storm away better.

"Yeah, you baby," Fiona says, mad at me instead of Jared, for some reason.

Me! And I didn't do anything.

I guess I'm not as scary as Jared, that's all—so Fiona can be braver against me.

I'm just EllRay Jakes, b-ball loser, who can't even get his goofy little hands on the ball once, much less shoot a basket.

And—**BZZ-Z-Z-Z!**

Just like that, recess is over.

✳ **2** ✳
PROMISES

"But Dad promised," I say to Mom in my darkened room that night. I am under the covers, and she is sitting on my quilt. Only the closet light is still on.

My dad is on a geology field trip in Arizona.

"Hmm," Mom replies. She sounds half-asleep, I think, frowning.

And this is important!

It is way past my bedtime, but I can't fall asleep. My dad's old orange Garfield clock ticks too loudly. Bare branches scratch at my bedroom window. They sound like the claws of the monster in my favorite handheld video game, *Die, Creature, Die*. It's like the monster is trying to get inside my room.

How does *anyone* sleep? Ever?

"Dad said I'd grow taller once the new year started," I say, hoping to wake Mom up a little. "And it's already February, but I'm not much closer to that basketball hoop than I was before Christmas. No one ever passes me the ball—even the kickball— unless recess is almost over and it doesn't count anymore. Or not even then! Not even Corey or Kevin pass to me. And they *like* me."

They are my two best friends at school—plus Marco, but he's not playing. Kevin is the only other boy in our class with brown skin like mine.

Why is basketball suddenly such a big deal to me?

1. For almost all the guys in my class, it's our latest thing. See, our school got two new basketballs for the playground in January, around the same time they finally fixed the hoops. They even got new heavy-duty nets, so it looks really cool out there.

2. And we're not like most girls, who—in my opinion—bounce from one fad to another every week, like the yoga thing I mentioned. This new b-ball thing is gonna stick.

3. Also, I have brown skin, like most famous basketball players do—which should give me at least a small head start, considering how rare brown skin is around here. Right?

4. So I should somehow make this thing happen.

"There are sports other than basketball, you know," Mom says. "And did your dad really promise you would grow this very year?" she asks, half teasing, as she pets my forehead with her cool fingers.

"Basically," I say.

Mom sighs. "But you must know that your father didn't mean you'd grow taller *right away* this year, honey-bun," she says. "He probably meant over the summer, or in the fall."

"I don't think it's ever gonna happen," I say. "I'm getting *left behind*. That's the point."

And it's the worst feeling in the world.

I have to be good at some sport to get respect at school, don't I?

And that's all I really need.

My best friend, Corey—the champion swimmer—has been looking taller and skinnier than ever since Christmas. And Marco is now taller than his main friend Major. Diego Romero has gotten taller since the holidays, too—and he was pretty tall to start with.

So unfair.

Even the girls are growing!

"I wish I could help you out," Mom says.

I scowl up at my bedroom ceiling, where a few fluorescent stars still glimmer: my private constellation. They're left over from when I was five, the year we moved to Oak Glen, California, from San Diego. It's an hour away if the traffic is good.

"Same stars as on the ceiling in your old room," my dad pointed out after sticking them up. "Same stars in the sky, too." He was trying to make me feel better about the move, I guess.

But even Professor Warren Jakes—also known as Dad—isn't perfect, I remind myself now. He would never *lie*, but he might have made one of his rare mistakes when he promised I'd grow taller this year.

After all, Alfie is a shrimp like me, isn't she? Maybe it runs in the family.

"*Beautiful elf*," her real name—Alfleta—means in some weird language only my mom has heard about, but that no one alive speaks anymore. And Alfie is kind of like an elf, I think, frowning some more. Tiny, stubborn, and all over the place.

Promises. Grown-ups are always promising something.

"EllRay, listen," Mom says, sounding wide awake now. "I'm quite tall, would you agree?"

I nod. She is taller than a lot of other Oak Glen moms. Prettier, too, I think, with her caramel-brown skin, her floaty scarves, and her perfect smile.

"And your dad's *very* tall," my mom continues. "And your doctor's not at all concerned that you won't grow," she adds, as if this is the winning argument. "He says you're perfectly normal, and that you'll shoot up like a weed when the time comes. Like a *weed*," she repeats, sounding impressed already.

As if weeds are so wonderful. And—she asked my *doctor*?

What am I, a medical emergency?

I think about it. "'Perfectly normal' isn't exactly *great*, Mom," I point out. "And weeds aren't very tall, are they? Most of them barely come up to your knees."

"They grow quickly once they get going, that's the point," my mom says, getting to her feet. "And you will grow, too."

"But when?" I ask.

Because what good will it be if I don't grow until I'm, like, seventeen?

I want respect *now*!

I want to be chosen first for stuff like basketball now!

Or chosen second or third, anyway. Not last.

"I'll ask your father to explain it to you again,

better, once he gets home from Arizona. Believe me," Mom says, making the promise as she turns off the closet light.

"No. That's okay," I say, my voice sounding hollow in the dark.

My dad loves explaining things, true. He is a college teacher, after all. But sometimes he explains things for so long—and in so much detail—that I actually forget what the question was. Or that I'm sorry I asked it in the first place.

And words alone—even really, really smart ones like my dad's—will never make me grow.

Neither will wishes. I've already tried wishing. Upon a star, even.

"Night, Mom," I say.

"Night," Mom says from the doorway. "See you in the morning."

"Yeah, the morning," I say to the now-empty room. "See you *shortly.*"

Well, of course.

EllRay "Shortly" Jakes. That's me.

3

REAL LIFE AT OAK GLEN PRIMARY SCHOOL

"It's a blustery day, so bundle up," Mom tells me the next morning, Wednesday, after she has dropped off Alfie at Kreative Learning and Daycare and driven me to school. I'm backing out of the car behind-first, like a dung beetle. Emma McGraw told me this is something they do. She wants to be a nature scientist when she grows up, so she knows weird stuff like that.

"Dung" means "poop," by the way. I am just reporting the facts.

"That jacket isn't only for show, honey-bun," my mother calls out as I haul both it and my backpack from the car.

Mom humor.

"I know. Bye, Mom," I say, glancing down the sidewalk. If Jared or Jared's sidekick Stanley

Washington hears her calling me "honey-bun," that will be my new nickname for a solid week.

At least.

Like the time Ms. Sanchez goofed and called me "sweetie" before Christmas. I'm still recovering from that one. I feel my cheeks get hot just thinking about it.

"*Ooh, it's Sweetie. Smoochy-smooch,*" Stanley said to me for days, slobbering over his hand as he pretend-kissed it. Even Jared finally told him to give it a rest.

I stand tall, as tall as possible, anyway, and put on my jacket. I hoist my bulging backpack over one skinny shoulder, and I lurch toward the playground.

With any luck, there will be no basketballs being used this morning.

"Dude," Corey calls out from the boys' picnic table, where he is eating a protein bar his mother packed—probably for his lunch. But lunch is many hours away.

Each picnic table is officially open to both boys

and girls, of course. But it doesn't work out that way in real life at Oak Glen Primary School.

I head toward Corey, who has close to three hundred freckles on his face. We tried to count them one rainy recess. I nod hi at Marco and Major as I pass.

"M and M," Ms. Sanchez sometimes calls them, they are so tight. But like I said, Marco is friends with me now, too. They're on the grass, playing olden days—dragons and knights—with some plastic figures Marco sneaked to school. Not that we usually break school rules such as "No toys from home," by the way. We only break the really goofy ones, the rules that make you start to wonder about the good ones—such as "No running in the halls," which just makes sense.

Have you seen how big some sixth-graders are? A third-grader could get smooshed! Not to mention a kindergartner.

But here is an example of an Oak Glen rule that does not make any sense. We are allowed to run on the playground when we are playing kickball or basketball, but we are *not* supposed to run just for the fun of it—because they say we might get hurt.

See what I mean?

"Hey," I tell Corey, giving him a friendly shove.

"Mmm," Corey greets me, his cheeks bulging. "Bring something fun?" he mumbles through his early morning snack.

"Not today," I tell him.

I was too busy getting mad about being short last night to figure out anything to bring. I would never sneak *Die, Creature, Die* to school, though. I could not risk having that confiscated—which means taken away from you by a grown-up. Maybe forever. Just the thought of everyone in the principal's office playing with my game makes me feel woozy.

I don't want them messing up my score, for one thing.

"What about playing rock-paper-scissors?" Corey asks after swallowing his mouthful of crumbs. "Best out of four. One, two, three, *go*."

1. First game: Me, scissors. Corey, rock. Rock smashes scissors. Corey wins.

2. Second game: Me, paper. Corey, rock. Paper wraps rock. I win.

3. Third game: Me, rock. Corey, rock. Again. So that
   one's a tie. Next one is the decider.
4. Fourth game: Me, scissors. Corey, paper. Scissors
   cut paper! I'm the ultimate winner!

Now, all I need is about a dozen more games
you can play sitting down. Because then, tallness
doesn't matter.

"Good one, EllRay," Corey says, smiling. He and
Kry are the best sports in our third grade class.

Emma and her friend Annie Pat Masterson are tied for third place in that category. Most of us other kids either *pretend* to be good sports, which Mom says is a perfectly fine thing to do, or else we "get our grouch on," as Ms. Sanchez sometimes says.

That means we get mad—and *stay* mad. For a while, anyway.

Girls stay mad the longest, in my opinion. It's like they have an extra gigabyte in their hard drives just for hurt feelings.

And speaking of Ms. Sanchez . . .

✳ **4** ✳

VOCABULARY BINGO

"Settle down, citizens," our teacher calls out after taking attendance.

"Citizens?" Ms. Sanchez is in a funny mood for a Wednesday!

"We're going to be trying something new today for Language Arts," she says, passing out pieces of poster board and plastic bags full of little squares with words pasted on them. "Cynthia's mother, Mrs. Harbison, made these for us," Ms. Sanchez says, making sure every kid gets one piece of poster board and one bag of words.

Cynthia wriggles in her seat and smirks, looking important.

Great, I think, hiding a sigh. All this class needs is one more thing for Cynthia to brag about at recess and lunch.

I examine what's in front of me. Hey, I think, smiling. This looks kind of like a game! The poster board is divided by marker lines into little squares, five rows down and five across. There's a spot marked "Free" in the middle. Each little square has a word on it, and a tiny piece of Velcro glued to it.

The little words in the bag have dabs of Velcro on their backs, too. I guess we're supposed to match words and stick them onto the poster board.

Alfie is gonna hate this Velcro game, if it's still around when she gets to Oak Glen Primary School. She will probably ask for a shoelace game instead.

"We're playing Vocabulary Bingo," Ms. Sanchez says, perching on the edge of her desk. "I will randomly choose some vocabulary words from our last few lists. You will match the words in your bags to the words on the poster board. The first one to get a straight line up and down or across calls out '*bingo.*' And he or she wins a prize."

"Is the prize food?" Corey asks, setting his words out on his desk with the precision of a Vocabulary Bingo master. He can be very neat when it counts, and food makes it count for him. It's his thing.

"Raise your hand before speaking, Corey," Ms. Sanchez reminds him. "This is a classroom, not some free-for-all. No, the prize is not food," she continues, answering his question. "It's something little but fun. A trinket, let's say."

"Trinkets are girl-toys," Jared mumbles to Stanley, but I think he's wrong about that. And I can tell he wants to win it anyway.

Jared Matthews is not that hard to figure out.

Heather's hand shoots up in the air like there's a cartoon bird attached to her wrist. "Is bingo the same as gambling?" she asks, looking pretend-worried, and as important as her friend Cynthia did a couple of minutes ago. The long skinny braid Heather wears for decoration swings across her face like a hairy exclamation mark. "Because I'm pretty sure gambling is against my religion," she informs us, bustling in her seat.

"We're not playing for money, Heather," Ms. Sanchez says, her foot swinging.

She wears really cute shoes, the girls all say. They vote on their favorites. "Don't you worry," our teacher assures Heather. "This is a religion-free vocabulary word game. Now, let's get started."

"Okay," Heather says, half under her breath. "I *guess.*"

And we begin. "*Eight,*" Ms. Sanchez says, loud and clear, after choosing a word from a sparkly decorated box Fiona gave her last Christmas. "As in, 'Some of you are still eight years old,'" she explains. "Pay attention, Marco," she adds.

I guess she doesn't want us to get the word

"eight" mixed up with "ate," which is also a good word. Just ask always-hungry Corey.

We all look down at our poster board squares, trying to find a word match.

"BINGO!" Jason calls out, super excited. He has buzz-cut hair, ears that stick out a little, and a chunky body that he claims is mostly muscle. He is also the closest thing we have to a class clown. But he's serious now.

Ms. Sanchez is shaking her head. "Five words down or across, Jason. In a *straight line*," she adds, as if guessing a future problem in advance.

"Dummy," Nate says, laughing.

"And that's name-calling," Ms. Sanchez says, smooth as can be. "Which means you will sit this game out, Mr. Marshall. I'm sorry about that. But please put your words away for now. Second word, everyone else—*light.* As in, 'Turn off the light.'"

And on we go.

This is surprisingly fun, I think, wrinkling my forehead so I don't miss any words. I don't even care that they're trying to trick us into learning stuff!

I feel kind of sorry for Nate, though. His red

rooster crest of hair is drooping, he's so miserable at being left out of the fun.

See, our class mostly looks out for each other. Nate forgot the rules for a second, that's all. He's still a good guy. Even Ms. Sanchez knows that—and Nate knows she still likes him as much as always.

And I'll share my trinket with him if I win—unless it's the temporary tattoo I spied on Ms. Sanchez's desk.

Because half a temporary tattoo would look pretty lame, wouldn't it?

✳ **5** ✳

TACO NIGHT!

"Oh boy," my little sister says, climbing up on a kitchen chair to watch Mom grate cheese. Alfie's three soft, puffy braids seem to be standing at attention, she's so excited.

Wednesday night is taco night at our house. Taco night! My favorite.

I don't know why we can't have foods kids like for dinner *every* night. Foods such as hamburgers, pizza, spaghetti and meatballs, grilled cheese sandwiches, corn-dogs, and peanut butter and jelly sandwiches with the crusts cut off. That, plus tacos, equals seven dinners. And there are seven nights in the week.

What would be so wrong about that?

Dad got home from his geology field trip late this morning, when I was at school. He's in the shower now, after taking a long afternoon nap. So we're all home together again. I like that feeling. It's just right, like finishing a jigsaw puzzle.

I am doing my homework at the kitchen table tonight, just in case any spoonfuls of taco meat need tasting, or there's a chunk of cheese left over after the grating. "Can I help?" Alfie asks Mom.

"The grater is too sharp for your precious little fingers," Mom says. "But you can fluff up the shredded lettuce, Alfie, if your hands are clean."

"Of course they're clean," Alfie says, insulted. "I'm not some *boy*."

"Hey," I object from the kitchen table. "That's not fair. Boys don't have dirty hands. Not all the time. And don't let her wreck the lettuce, Mom."

I have been looking forward to this dinner all day.

"Boys have dirty hands at *my* school, EllWay," Alfie says, fluffing away. "Like Scooter Davis," she adds. Lettuce is flying all over the counter.

"EllWay" is "EllRay" in Alfie-speak. And I guess Scooter is a new kid in Alfie's daycare. I haven't heard her talk about him before, anyway.

"No boys are coming to my kindergarten party,"

Alfie adds under her breath. "But we're gonna have tacos, and cupcakes, and pink punch with floating cherries. And the best goodie bags in the world. And it's gonna be *here*."

"What kindergarten party?" Mom asks. "You're still in preschool, sweetie-pie. And try to keep the lettuce in the bowl."

But Mom never really gets mad about spills and stuff like that. She's more of a big-deal kind of mom, like when I get a "Needs Improvement" note on a progress report, or when Alfie loses her sneakers in the library.

My dad's like that, too—only more so. I mean, he gets worked up a little faster.

"What party, Alfie?" Mom asks again, stirring a packet of taco seasoning powder into the sizzling meat, and then sloshing in a little water from the teakettle sitting on the stove. "What party?" she says for the third time, but in a cooler tone of voice. Mom turns to face Alfie, who is chewing on a shred of lettuce the size of a blade of grass. Alfie points to her mouth, as if showing how busy it is. Too busy for talking.

And, "No talking when you're chewing." That's one of Mom's rules.

Alfie finally swallows, in a fakey kind of way. "I just meant if we ever *gave* a party," she explains, changing her story as she goes along. "Like a kindergarten party. You know," she says. "To practice for starting primary school next year so we won't look like babies. It would be mostly for my friends, because they're so worried about it," she adds, like her kindness will win Mom over.

Alfie has three main friends at Kreative Learning and Daycare. Suzette Monahan, Arletty, and Mona. The three of them always seem to be either celebrating, feuding, or plotting how to get even for something. It's hard to keep track.

The point is, their feelings are just like regular, older people's feelings—but looked at under one of Dad's science microscopes. Every little thing becomes *huge*.

What is Alfie up to now?

"You're having a Valentine's Day party at daycare," Mom says, as if Alfie needs reminding. She already has her outfit all planned. "And your birthday party was last June," Mom continues. "Remember the bouncy castle? So don't go getting your hopes up about having another party anytime soon, lovie. Not here. Your dad's going to be extra busy for a month or two, and I have a deadline coming up."

My mom writes books for grown-up ladies about the days when people were named Alfleta and Lancelot.

Yes, Lancelot Raymond Jakes is my real name. But I changed it to EllRay as soon as I could talk.

"What-*ever*," Alfie says, shrugging in a sulky way as she stares down at the lettuce bowl, which looks like it just erupted on the counter.

I've heard Suzette say "what-*ever*" before. And our babysitter says it, too, when she's talking on her cell. That's probably where Alfie got it.

Mom's eyes narrow, and one hand parks itself on her hip. "You know I don't care for that expression, Miss Alfie," she says in a voice that has turned a tiny bit scary. "It's disrespectful. And you are not some reality show teenager who doesn't know any better."

Alfie—who can be kind of a drama queen, or a drama princess, at least—sighs.

But she doesn't say "what-*ever*" again.

"The lettuce looks fine," Mom says in a fake-cheerful voice, trying to get things back to where they were a few minutes ago. "Put it in the fridge, would you, EllRay?"

"Yeah," Alfie mumbles, taking it out on me. "Put it in the fwidge, EllWay. I *command* you."

"*Mom*," I object.

But after one look at Mom's face, I get up and put the bowl of shredded lettuce in the fridge, ignoring my little sister in a big way the whole time.

If she wants to be a pain, let her.

I'm not gonna let it ruin taco night, that's for sure!

✳ **6** ✳

NEGATIVE NUMBERS

A couple of hours later, Dad pokes his head into my room just before bedtime. "Your little sister wants to talk to you, son," he tells me. "She says it's urgent."

"I thought she was already asleep," I say, stretching.

Bath-time, story time, and bedtime are such big deals with Alfie each night that our entire family gets worn out. Well, everyone except Alfie.

It was never like that when I was her age. Even Mom says so. I would just sneak a small car or action figure to bed with me and whisper to it until I fell asleep.

Alfie's more "high maintenance," my dad says.

That's a fancy way of saying spoiled, in my opinion. No offense to Alfie, except she makes it such a big deal when she doesn't get her way that we all cave in. But she didn't spoil *herself*, even Mom sometimes says.

When Alfie is under the covers at last, it's as if Mom, Dad, and I are very hard workers who have finally been allowed to take a break. Or maybe we're like the grown-ups at Oak Glen Primary School when they slip into the Teachers' Lounge.

I was all relaxed until Dad said Alfie wants to talk to me. Well, as relaxed as a person can be when he is supposed to be "comparing negative numbers" for math homework.

Yes, that's a real thing.

And I have learned how to do it, even though it doesn't make any sense.

That's what a lot of school is like, if you ask me.

"Do I *have* to talk to Alfie?" I ask Dad. "I already played horsie with her for ten minutes after her bath. And I'm kind of busy here," I tell him, ruffling my worksheet a little. "Negative numbers," I add, like they're piling up fast—in an invisible empty bucket, maybe.

"Better just get it over with," he advises, shaking his head. "This situation is not going away."

"So what's up?" I ask, padding barefoot into Alfie's pink-and-purple bedroom, now lit only by a glowing sparkly plastic flower that my mom plugged into an outlet on the wall.

Alfie is sitting up in bed, pillows all over the place. "Shh," she whispers, peering at the door, as if Mom and Dad might be hiding behind it, trying to get in on this.

Mm-hmm.

"Close the door, EllWay," my sister says. "I have to tell you something important. It's about my kindergarten party."

"Which you're not having," I remind her. But I take a seat at the very end of her bed—between a couple of stuffed animals. A unicorn and a dolphin.

Alfie thinks unicorns are real and dolphins aren't real, by the way. Just to give you some idea of the way her brain works.

"And I don't even want a party," Alfie says. "Not *here,* even though I do wanna start practicing for being a kindergarten girl. But I don't like parties at home. You know that! Because at parties, I have to share my toys."

It's true. That's one of our mom's rules—though she lets us put a couple of toys away before kids come over, if we really need to. But just one or two things.

"I like parties to be at school," Alfie explains. "Or at the pizza place. Or at the movies. Not here."

"So why are you bugging Mom and Dad to let you have a party here?" I ask.

"Because this is where it would have to be," Alfie says, as if she is giving me a good explanation. "I already told Suzette she can't come! And that means she will never be able to play with my new horsie barn. But you can't tell Mom the part about Suzette and the horsie barn. That's our deal."

It's true. We keep each other's secrets. We are on the same team.

"Wait a minute," I say, holding up a hand. "You want to have a party here, at home, where you don't even like having parties—just so Suzette Monahan can't come to it?"

Alfie nods. "And I already *told* her she can't

come. So she will never, ever be able to play with my new horsie barn," she explains once more. "*Or* get the best goodie bag ever. *Or* get to pretend she's in kindergarten. And it serves her wight."

"*Right.*"

I skip over a few of the obvious things wrong with Alfie's plan, such as the fact that she doesn't even *have* a new barn yet for her plastic horses, she just wants one. And there aren't any goodie bags lying around the house—because there isn't going to *be* a party, whether Alfie wants one or not.

Which she doesn't, not really.

But instead of pointing out these obvious flaws in her plan, I ask my sister a question. "Why did you tell Suzette she can't come to your party?"

"To be mean to her before she's mean to me," Alfie explains.

Like, "*Duh.*"

"I decided it on Monday," she adds, as if that's why it makes sense.

I think for a few seconds, trying to figure out whether or not this is a good example of negative numbers in action.

1. Take one party that is not going to happen—here or anywhere.
2. Subtract one little girl, Suzette, who is not invited to come to that party.
3. Then, whatever happens, do not allow Suzette to play with the plastic horse barn we don't even own.
4. Finally, take away the best goodie bag ever, one that does not yet exist.
5. And do all these mean things so Suzette can't be mean to Alfie first.

"Has Suzette been mean to you at daycare?" I ask, frowning. Because Suzette Monahan can be mean. Bossy, anyway. And not only at daycare! The first time she came over to our house for a play date last fall, Suzette told my mom they had to go to McDonald's when it was snack time.

And Mom had made cookies and everything!

There was lots of noise when Mom said no to Suzette, too. In fact, when she's talking about Alfie's friends to Dad, Mom secretly calls Suzette "Uproar Girl." I've heard her say it.

"Suzette hasn't been mean *lately*," Alfie admits,

scowling in the gloom. "Not to me. But she's gonna try to boss me around next year . . . I just know it. But if you're mean to people before they can be mean to you, then they can't be mean to you first. Because you already did it. And then maybe she'll leave me alone in kindergarten."

Like—**TA-DA!**

"But—but that's just wrong, Alfie," I sputter. "And maybe it's the same thing as being a bully," I add, already knowing she won't get what I'm trying to say.

Alfie thinks she is making perfect sense.

And that unicorns are real.

"Suzette's the bully," Alfie informs me.

"Maybe *usually* she is. A little bit, at least," I half-agree. "But this time, you're kind of the one who's being the—"

"*She's* the bully," Alfie insists. "And I'm the nice one. And you're the brother of the nice one. And you're gonna get Mom and Dad to have my kindergarten party here at our house, because—"

"Because you already told Suzette she can't come," I say, finishing her sentence.

"So she can't be mean to me first," Alfie says, correcting me.

Correcting me being one of her favorite things to do.

"I'm sorry to tell you this," I tell my elf-like little sister, who is in danger of turning into a preschool thug. "But your kindergarten party is flat-out not gonna happen."

"For reals?" Alfie asks, her eyes wide.

"Mom already told you," I remind her. "Sorry, Alf."

"But don't tell Mom about Suzette, okay?" she says. "Because that's my secret—with you."

This, on top of my own problems.

Lucky me!

7

GOSSIP

"Guess what?" Cynthia Harbison says the next morning before school. We are all out by the picnic tables. "I heard some gossip," she announces. Cynthia takes off her pink plastic headband, smoothes back her hair, then puts the toothy headband back on so tight that it looks like her hair hurts.

As usual, the girls are at one of their own picnic tables, and us boys are at one of ours. But we can hear each other talk.

"What's gossip?" Major asks Marco.

"It's like when you tell a lie," Marco says, keeping his voice low.

"Naw," Jared says, louder. He shakes his head. "Gossip is when you talk smack about someone."

"Talking smack" means putting someone down. Like, *"He's so little you gotta put rocks in his pocket when it's windy out, or he'll blow away."*

Jared said that about me once, so I guess he's the smack-talking expert around here.

It was supposed to be a joke.

"Yeah. It's talkin' smack," his sidekick Stanley agrees. Big surprise.

Jared is only eight years old, like the rest of us. And he lives in Oak Glen, in a very nice house. But one of his favorite things to do is talk like some tough guy in a rap video.

"That's not even right, *boys*," Heather calls out from the girls' table. Her skinny little decoration-braid swings across her face. "Gossip is when you tell a friend something about someone else," she continues. "Even if you're not all-the-way sure it's true."

"Why say it, then?" Corey asks.

"Because *maybe* it's true," Fiona says. Sticking up for gossip, I guess.

"And this gossip is *all-the-way* true," Cynthia says. "Because I heard my mom talking on the phone. Except it's more boy-gossip than girl-gossip, so who really cares? I was just trying to be nice, telling you guys."

"Us guys don't even care," Jason says in a loud, bored voice.

"Huh," Cynthia scoffs. "Even when the gossip is about you getting your own special basketball coach? Starting today, Thursday? Pre-basketball, anyway."

"Probably because they're so terrible at the real thing," Heather says, shaking her head in pretend pity.

"Okay. What does 'pre' mean?" Major asks Marco, like he's about to give up on definitions for the day. Two of them already—and class hasn't even started yet!

But Marco is off in his own daydreamy world again, scraping gunk off the picnic table with a plastic spoon. I don't know what he plans to do with it. Nothing, I hope.

"'Pre' means 'before,'" Diego Romero tells Major. "Like, 'preschool' happens before you go to regular school," he explains. Diego reads a lot.

And suddenly, it feels as though my head is spinning—like a basketball on a professional player's giant finger. Because what in the world is *pre-basketball*? Anything could come before basketball! Or b-ball, as us guys call it.

1. Getting out of the car in front of school could be "pre-basketball."
2. So could running—I mean walking—onto the playground.
3. Or trying to grab one of the new balls.

Why would a kid need lessons in any of those things?

"Just the boys get to have a coach?" Kry asks Cynthia. "That's not fair. *I* like basketball, too." Her brown eyes look fierce behind her shiny, straight bangs.

"And I'll try it if Kry does it. I'm tired of yoga," Emma McGraw says, even though she's the shortest girl in our class. But she's still taller than I am.

See what I mean about "no fair" when it comes to height?

Cynthia bites her lip for a second, because Kry is the only girl in our class who she's a little bit afraid of. Not because Kry is mean. Just the opposite!

Everyone likes Kry, so she's a puzzle Cynthia cannot figure out.

"I'm sure they might let you play if you *want*," she finally says, shrugging.

"Yeah, maybe. If you *want*," Heather says, like it sounds pretty dumb to her.

All this maybe-talk, gossip-talk has gone on long enough. "*Who* is gonna let them play? Let *us* play, I mean," I say. "Who's the coach gonna *be*? We don't even have any coaches at Oak Glen Primary. We don't have teams! So I think you're just—"

"It's Mr. Havens," Cynthia interrupts, triumphant. "He's real good at basketball, it turns out. He was on a team in college. So *ha-ha*, EllRay Jakes. You're wrong, wrong, wrong!"

Mr. Havens.

The second grade teacher, brand-new to Oak Glen this year.

The man who substitutes for the recess monitor—more and more, lately.

I've even gotten in trouble with him before. Accidentally, of course.

"Huh," my sometimes-friend Kevin snort-says. "Mr. Havens is always too busy passing out kickballs and taking care of nosebleeds and skinned knees to coach anyone."

"And he keeps kids from walking up the slide, too,

which is perfectly safe and fun," Jared complains, as if he's had some personal experience with this.

Which he has.

"The regular playground monitor will take care of that stuff," know-it-all Cynthia says. "And Mr. Havens is gonna coach the—the pre-basketball kids."

HA! She almost said "the boys."

"He's volunteering, even," Cynthia adds, kind of mad at us now. "Because Mr. Havens told Principal James that he can't stand seeing you guys just running around in circles with the new basketballs. Missing baskets, bouncing the balls wrong, and breaking official rules. And Principal James told my mother that, over the phone, because she's in charge of making sure us Oak Glen kids get more exercise at school."

Oh, yeah? Who made fancy Mrs. Harbison the Queen of Exercise? She's always wearing high heels! Let's see *her* shoot some hoops.

"And you were listening in on her," Stanley says, triumphant.

"Snoopy-snoopy-snoop," Kevin jeers.

"I'm pretty sure listening in on phone calls is

against the law," Diego says, his forehead wrinkling as he thinks.

"Only if you get caught," Heather snaps.

"I heard what they said by accident," Cynthia says, defending herself. "I just thought you guys would like to know, that's all. *You're welcome*," she adds, her voice full of sarcasm.

Sarcasm is a specialty of hers. Alfie could take lessons.

"If you're even right," Kevin mumbles as the buzzer for class sounds.

Hmm, I think, hauling my backpack onto my knobbly shoulder once more. I wonder if she *is* right?

A basketball coach! That would be very, very cool. Even if it is Mr. Havens, who maybe already hates me.

Cool, except for the part where I'm still the shortest kid in my class. Mr. Havens won't even be interested in a shrimp like me.

But on the other hand, he's gotta help my pre-basketball skills a little, at least.

It's not like they can get any worse!

And—I am smiling as I walk into Ms. Sanchez's third grade class.

8

PRE-BASKETBALL

"Mr. Havens will work with all third-graders interested in pre-basketball during recess on Monday, Wednesday, and Thursday mornings," Ms. Sanchez tells us right before we go outside for morning recess. "And a few rare afternoons as well. It's a good thing you and the second-graders have recess at the same time."

"What's Mr. Havens doing on Tuesday and Friday?" Nate asks after Ms. Sanchez calls on him. "Because we wanna get really good at pre-basketball. We should practice every day."

"Yeah," Major says. "We want to get all the way to b-ball, without the *pre*."

"Mr. Havens will probably be busy lying down in the Teachers' Lounge on Tuesdays and Fridays, with an ice pack on his aching back," Ms. Sanchez says, laughing. "We'll see how long he can keep this up."

If Ms. Sanchez weren't already engaged to be married to her boyfriend, Mr. Timberlake, who runs a sporting goods store, I'm sure the girls in our class would already have paired her up with Mr. Havens. Mr. Havens is very tall, and he has one of those muscle-necks where the shirt barely buttons, and a head shaped like an almost-perfect rectangle. His hair is shaved into a fade at the sides, but there's a squiggle of red-blond hair up top.

He looks like a Canadian Mountie, the cartoon hero kind.

Cynthia says Mr. Havens is already married, even though he doesn't wear a wedding ring.

Girls know stuff like that. They can just tell.

Us boys don't care if he's married or not. We just want him to be a good coach.

"Move it," Jared says a few minutes later, elbowing Corey aside as he speed-walks down Oak Glen

Primary School's crowded main hall. We are eager to get outside for our first pre-basketball coaching session. Even the kids who don't want to play are making tracks—because they want to watch. This is something new.

And how often does something new happen at school on a Thursday?

In *February*?

I am so excited! I have forgotten all my worries about negative numbers, and about how my little sister Alfie—who, face it, is kind of my responsibility—is turning into a Kreative Learning and Daycare monster, and about me still being the shortest kid in my class. Even though it's a brand new year, and Dad promised I would grow.

Well, I've *almost* forgotten all those things.

Because now it's time to meet Mr. Havens in person! I've met him before, of course—on the playground. And it hasn't always been in the best way. It's usually after some scuffle I accidentally got trapped in. Nothing serious, though.

But I've never met Mr. Havens as an official pre-basketball coach. Maybe he can teach me some crazy-good skills that will help make up for how short I am!

This is *so different.*

"Yay!" a bunch of us yell as we erupt onto the playground for our first pre-basketball coaching session.

This is gonna be *awesome.*

9

COACH

FWE-E-E-ET! Mr. Havens's silver whistle blows, as we churn our way over to him like a school of third grade fish. A big net bag full of balls—basketballs and kickballs—is at his feet.

"Line up for your drills, boys and girls," Mr. Havens shouts, clapping his big hands twice. Not that he doesn't already have our attention. "We only have twenty minutes together," he says. "So, two straight lines—facing each other. Now!"

We form our lines. It's mostly boys, but Kry, Emma, and Annie Pat are in the group, too. I think Kry's the one who will stick it out. She's good at sports.

"Eyes on me, everyone," Mr. Havens says. "You probably know me as Mr. Havens, but during these training sessions, you will call me Coach. Say 'Coach.'"

"Coach," a few of us mumble.

"Louder," he says.

"*Coach!*" we all shout.

"That's better," he says. "Remember, this isn't a tea party. Now, here's your go-to stance," Coach tells us. "I want your legs a shoulders' width apart, one foot forward for balance. And your knees are a little bent at all times. Your weight should be on the front of your feet—the part up by your toes—so you can move fast and jump. Like this," he says, demonstrating. "Take the stance!" he shouts.

And we do it. We try, anyway. But Corey crouches down so low that he looks like he's about to dive off a board at the Aquatics Center. Jason goes up so far on his toes that he looks as if he's gonna fall over. And Jared's feet are way too far apart. It looks more like a movie monster's stance than a basketball player's.

Marco looks like he wishes he were someplace else. Is he gonna hurl? He shoots me a glance that says *"Help,"* but I don't know what to do about it.

Instead, I correct my own stance, looking at other kids' mistakes. And Mr. Havens—"Coach"—prowls up and down the middle of our two lines, making adjustments here and there.

"Okay, good," he finally says. "Remember, that's your go-to stance. As in *always*. And now for a ball-handling drill. Fingertips on the ball, players. *Fingertips!* Not your hands. Got that?"

"Fingertips," we robot-repeat as he scoops a ball out of the net bag and demonstrates how to hold it.

"Like your hand is a spider," he tells us. "Practice this at home, if you can—with both hands. It'll get easier as you grow."

And I'm thinking, *They do this?* Because on TV, you don't notice b-ball players holding the ball that way. They're moving around so fast, or dribbling, which I already know is another word for bouncing the ball—not slobbering on the floor. You have to dribble the ball to move it around on the court. You can't just grab the ball and run.

But the fingertips thing is good, because my fingertips are as big as any other third grade kid's. Fingertips don't care how tall you stand.

"Here are the balls we have to work with," Coach says, tossing them to us fast. "Here! Here! Here! Basketballs, kickballs. Doesn't matter. Catch them with your fingertips, and then throw them to the kid facing you. Now! Now!"

This guy is not fooling around.

✳ **10** ✳

LIKE BIG KIDS

I somehow nab a partly deflated kickball with my spider fingertips. I look across from me. "Kevin," I say. "Heads up." And I toss him the ball. He catches it.

So far, so good, even though all that means is that I haven't made a fool of myself. *Yet.*

"Fingertips, people," Coach reminds us again. "And use both hands, Marco! The ball's not gonna bite you. Keep those balls moving, guys. Now! Now! Now!"

"When do we get to shoot baskets?" Nate asks.

"When you're ready," Coach says. "Which is *not now.* Next, some dribble drills. You're going to start bouncing that ball waist-high, then work it down to the ground. Like this," he says.

And he starts bouncing his demonstration

basketball, moving around the whole time, knees bent. "Watch my footwork," he says. He's fast!

Bounce. Bounce. Bounce. Bounce.

Bounce-bounce-bounce-bounce.

Bouncebouncebouncebouncebounce.

At the end, his basketball is about two inches off the blacktop as he dribbles it. He even moves in a complete circle around the ball. He's bouncing the ball so fast that it looks like it's glued to the bottom of his hand.

Whoa.

"Okay. Go!" Coach says, and a bunch of us start dribbling our balls.

BOUNCE. BOUNCE. BOUNCE.

"Hey. I don't even *have* a ball," Stanley says, hands on his hips. He's mad!

"Only half of you do," Coach says, pointing out the obvious. "I want the rest of you to run in place— on the balls of your feet. But keep your stance. Then you'll swap places with the dribblers."

And a little bit of running in place starts to happen. But not a lot.

"I'm not doin' that," Jared mutters, watching

Major and even the reluctant Marco spring from foot to foot, real fast. "It looks dumb, yo."

It's like Coach has superpower hearing. "Bad attitudes get to run laps around the playground," he announces, not even looking at Jared. "Or they can forget the whole thing and go play on the teeter-totters and eat fruit leathers with the little kids. Good times."

And—Jared starts to run in place.

I think we are all starting to like Coach. He's tough, but that's because he's treating us like big kids, not babies.

"Now switch," Coach says. "Dribblers, pass the balls—and start running in place. But keep your stance! And bend your knees. No Frankenstein clomping on my watch."

And I run, even though a fruit leather is sounding pretty good to me right now.

So far, the three best dribblers are Corey, Diego, and Kry. But Emma's having trouble bouncing the ball waist-high more than three or four times without it *boing*-ing off in some weird direction.

Wow! I'm better than someone at dribbling!

I feel bad for Emma, but I can't help but feel a little happy for me.

"Now slow it down," Coach says after a few more switches. "Slower, slower, slower. And dribblers, bring that ball back *up-p-p* to your waist, if you can. Runners, shake out those crazy legs. Time to cool down."

"I'm already freezing," Stanley complains.

"That's probably because you weren't running fast enough," Coach tells him. "'Cooling down' means slowly getting your muscles back to normal— like by walking around a little. Now listen, boys and girls," he says. "We're not meeting again until Monday morning. Any of you have basketballs at home? Or kickballs? Or even beach balls? Just about anything this size," he says, holding his own basketball up high on one finger while it spins.

Whoa!

Most hands go up in the air, including mine.

"That ball is your new best friend," Coach informs us. "You play with it over the weekend—with your fingertips, remember. Even when you watch TV, but *carefully.* Just toss that sucker from hand to hand. Because you guys are two-handed players, am I right?"

"You're right," we chorus, trying to picture what he means.

"You are *not* gonna say, '*Oh, wait a minute, other team. Throw the ball to my good hand, okay?*' Are you?" he asks, using a funny voice when he's pretending to be the goofy, one-handed player.

"No way," we shout.

I think Jared even added "sir." Like he thinks he's in the army, maybe.

"Okay then," Coach says. "Balls back in the bag, people. Quick! Quick! Quick!"

And just as the last ball goes into the big net bag, the buzzer sounds.

How did Coach *know* that?

We kind of shuffle back to class. My legs are numb, but they feel good.

I feel good.

"Didn't Coach say there was gonna be a tea party?" I hear Annie Pat ask Emma.

"Nuh-uh," Emma says, shaking her curly head.

"He said this *wasn't* a tea party. Remember?"

"Oh, yeah," Annie Pat says. And her red pigtails droop.

I kinda know how she feels. I could use two or three minutes at the drinking fountain, that's for sure. Even though the water there always tastes funny.

But this—this was fun!

✻ 11 ✻

IS THIS HOW IT STARTS?

"Put down that ball. It's bothering me," Alfie says during Saturday morning cartoons. It was her turn to choose them this week, so we are watching *Mimi Sparkle Kitties*, her new favorite. It's Japanese anime for little kids. Anime cartoons have those big-eyed guys in them.

It is a cloudy Saturday. It's almost dark out, even though it's nine in the morning. You can just tell it's about to start pouring in a few minutes. It's like that in California, Dad says. There's no rain for months, and then it floods.

But maybe our family will get to go to a movie together this wet afternoon!

Sweet.

"Put that down," Alfie says again, like she's the main Mimi Sparkle Kitty, the one with the biggest eyes, and I am just here to obey her.

That Mimi Sparkle Kitty scowls a lot, but in a cute way. She wears a little sailor suit, for some reason. But you can tell she's a girl because of the bow in her spiky pink fur.

"I *can't* put the ball down," I tell Alfie, passing it from hand to hand—fingertips!—as fast as I can. "This basketball is my new best friend," I say, quoting Coach.

"It's just a kickball," Alfie reminds me. "And kiss it, if you love it so much," she adds, hurling one of Mom's many throw pillows at me. "That's what Suzette says at school," she informs me, as if that makes it okay to repeat.

Suzette Monahan. Right.

Why am I so worried about defending Suzette? She's worse than Alfie, usually.

I dodge that pillow using only a tiny pinch of my new athletic skills. And I don't miss a beat with the ball. *Back, forth. Back, forth. Back, forth.*

My left hand is getting stronger, I think!

"Quit it, EllWay," Alfie says, reaching for another pillow.

"Your show's back on," I tell her. "I think the Mimi Sparkle Kitties are about to get in a fight with those blue dogs."

Back, forth. Back, forth.

Alfie's eyes are on the TV screen again.

"Maybe the Sparkle Kitties won't let the dogs come to their pretend kindergarten party," I tease. "Then they can't practice printing their names and paying attention."

BOOM! A sudden clap of thunder almost shakes the house, and hard drops of rain hit the windows like tiny BBs. "See?" Alfie says, still watching TV. "That's what you get, EllWay. And my party should have been happening tomowwow."

Tomorrow. "Sunday?" I ask.

"Yeah. Sunday," Alfie says. "That's what I told Suzette, anyway. But nobody else," she adds. She only looks a little bit worried.

How goofed-up is she, anyway? Alfie is acting like she still thinks it's happening, even though Mom said no!

Alfie twirls the curly end of one of her three soft braids as she watches a Sparkle Kitty dressed like a sailor-ninja creep closer to a sleeping dog. "So *ha-ha* on Suzette," she says, smiling a little. "She'll be sad all day."

My sister's face barely changes expression when she says that.

Geez, what a brat. What happened to my nice little sister?

"Listen," I say. "That's not cool, Alf—making Suzette sad. What's up with that?"

I really want to know. Is Alfie turning mean?

Is this how it starts? Almost by accident?

And if so, what am I gonna do to stop it?

She's my responsibility! The part of her that plays with other kids is, anyway.

I know way more about that than Mom and Dad. It's my *area*.

Alfie just twirls her hair some more. I try to figure out the many ways of messing up and being mean, thinking about which is the worst.

1. First, being mean–on–purpose is always worse than being mean–by–accident, in my opinion. For example, some random kid in your class might hear you talking about a sleepover they're not invited to. That's too bad, but it's an accident. You

can make it right. You could apologize, or even invite the kid to come over. To the sleepover, if it's your party, or some other time.

2. But if you tell them *on purpose* that they're not invited, that's mean.

3. And if you totally invent some party just to make a kid feel bad about not being invited, the way Alfie did with Suzette, that's even worse. Maybe it's even bullying.

4. All three times, the left-out kid would feel bad, so there isn't much difference there.

5. But *what you meant to do to the kid* is the big difference, I think. And that counts for a lot! I don't think Alfie gets that yet, though.

This is kind of a new way of thinking, even for me. Alfie couldn't figure it out if she had to. Maybe tossing the basketball is improving my mind! Speeding things up a little.

But in this case, Alfie is failing the test big-time. She *wants* Suzette to feel sad all day. That's why she hasn't personally canceled her imaginary party yet.

What can I do to help my little sister, though?

✳ **12** ✳

GETTING IT ALL WRONG

"You're *not* telling Mom," Alfie says during the next commercial, like that's the theme song to her own personal TV show.

And *"That's our deal!"* is her motto.

"Maybe I will tell, and maybe I won't," I say, shrugging.

But I probably won't tell.

There's a chance that keeping secrets should *not* be our deal, though. Because what if Alfie really is turning into the baby version of a mean girl, or bully-in-training, and she came up with some really goofy—even dangerous—plan, and she told me not to blab? Just because it's "our deal"?

That would be a problem. A deal-breaker, even.

Alfie's old stunts used to be more like swiping a couple of cookies from the kitchen, or sneaking into Mom's closet to try on her high heels, or hiding the sweater Grandmama sent that she didn't want to wear. Not making another little girl cry all day for no reason.

Even Suzette Monahan probably has feelings.

I mean, it's *possible*.

Suddenly, Mom is in the room. She holds her cell phone high in the air, like it is proof of something.

She does not look happy.

"Guess," she says to Alfie and me. "*Guess*."

I don't think we're really supposed to guess anything, strangely enough.

"Mrs. Monahan just called me," Mom says, charging right into her news like a pro

basketball player dribbling his way down the court.

Or her way.

"Mrs. Monahan is Suzette's mother," Mom reminds us. "And she was really upset that Suzette was not invited to Alfie's kindergarten party. Her imaginary party, that is. I actually had to *apologize* to the woman," Mom adds. I can tell how much her mouth hates saying those words. Still holding the cell, her hands go to her hips, which usually means trouble. "Well?" Mom says, waiting.

"Alfie's over there," I say, and I point my newly athletic finger in my sister's direction.

"You told Mom what I did?" Alfie shouts, giving me the stink-eye as she springs to her feet.

"No! I—"

"You *knew* about this?" Mom asks me. "EllRay Jakes, I expect better from you."

"*Me?*"

"You *told*," Alfie says, scowling like the fiercest Mimi Sparkle Ninja-Soldier Kitty in the world.

"You should have informed me, EllRay," Mom says. "If you knew."

So now each one's mad at me for no reason. Or for opposite reasons.

I don't know what to say. "May I please be excused?" I ask after about a thousand seconds.

"You may," Mom tells me. "I need to talk to Miss Alfie, here, about letting her imagination run away with her—just because she wanted a party. And I'll talk to you later, young man."

You're getting it all wrong, Mom, I try to tell Mom without saying any words. *That's not even the worst of what Alfie was trying to do!*

But my silent communication skills don't seem to be working.

And I'm not blabbing. Not yet, anyway.

So I scoop up my fake basketball, now my *only* friend in the house, not counting Dad. He is probably doing the hard Saturday crossword puzzle in the kitchen, so we can't disturb him. And I leave the room.

As fast—and as tall—as I can.

✳ **13** ✳

THE MOVING SIDEWALK

"Am I in big trouble for not telling you guys about Alfie's kindergarten party?" I ask Dad the next night, Sunday. It is still raining, but it is warm and cozy inside—except for the cold, nervous feeling in my stomach.

Mom is upstairs giving Alfie her endless bath, and Dad and I are hanging out in the family room. There's a nature show on TV, but the sound is off.

"There was never going to be any party," Dad says. "And kindergarten is months and months away," he reminds me, adjusting his glasses as he glances at the screen.

"Yes," I say, wanting to agree with him. "So there was nothing to tell, right?" I toss my ball back and forth a few times, wishing the new strength in my fingertips could spread to the rest of me. Then I'd be better able to face The Wrath of Dad—if he's mad at me, that is.

Sometimes it's hard to tell with him.

The main thing is, I do not want Dad to take away my handheld video game, *Die, Creature, Die.* That's my worst punishment.

"It's not quite that simple, son," he says, turning to look at me like I'm some interesting new specimen. Or almost-interesting, anyway. "You knew what was going on with your sister, EllRay, yet you said nothing. And please put down that ball. It's distracting."

Good, I think—because I need all the help I can get in this conversation.

But of course I put down the ball. "Sorry," I say. "It's just that Coach said he wants us to be two-handed players. We're supposed to handle the ball all weekend."

"Which you have done," Dad says. "And who is 'Coach,' by the way?"

"Mr. Havens," I tell him. "He started teaching second grade this year, but he used to be on the basketball team in college. He volunteered to help us third-graders learn how to play better."

"That was good of him," Dad says, nodding his approval.

"It would be better if I had a *real basketball*," I say, looking down at the kickball on the rug. "And no offense, but this family could use a basketball hoop, too," I add. "Above our garage door."

This fancy footwork–style hint might distract him from being mad at me.

"I know where basketball hoops go," Dad says. "I may not be the world's biggest expert on the sport, son—or even very interested in it. But I'm interested in what interests *you*."

"Well, I wish we had a ball and a hoop," I say, trying not to back down. My heart is pounding, though. I can't think fast enough to say something nice back to him.

Even though there are lots of good things I could say.

"That's not a totally impossible wish," Dad says, half smiling. "But sometimes it's hard to keep up with all your interests, EllRay. I don't think you ever even *mentioned* basketball until a couple of weeks ago."

"Because that's when us guys started playing it," I say.

"But you can't expect sports equipment simply to appear out of the blue," Dad says. "Let's give the game some time, and see if you're still interested in a month or so."

"I will be," I insist, folding my arms across my chest. "Or I will be if I ever grow tall enough," I mumble.

"Yes. Your mom told me you were still worried about that," Dad says.

"Because you said I would grow this year," I remind him. "You *promised*."

Like I already said, it's not so much the height thing as it is the *respect* I need—for being good at something. That's the problem. But it is way too hard to explain.

"It's only February, son," Dad says. "There's still plenty of time left in the year. I think I was your age when I had my growth spurt. Or I was nine or ten, anyway."

"Growth spurt." That sounds kind of weird, doesn't it?

Wait. "Nine or ten?" I yelp. "That's *years* from now, Dad! You mean like the fifth grade? I'll be a whole different person!"

"You'll be the same EllRay Jakes, believe me," Dad says, laughing. "Growing taller is not like climbing stairs, where you just go up, up, up, one step at a time until you're grown, or like being on an escalator. Instead, sometimes you reach what's called a plateau."

"And plateaus are flat," I say, remembering some of the geology stuff my dad has taught me.

"That's right," Dad says, pleased. "And at those times, it's more like you're on a moving sidewalk for a while, instead of climbing stairs. A moving sidewalk? Like at the airport?" he says, looking at me to see if I'm getting it.

"I remember," I say.

"You're not climbing, but you are moving forward," Dad explains anyway. "Maybe those are the times when you're growing on the inside, son. And then suddenly, you start climbing again. More stairs."

"But you're saying I'm on the moving sidewalk

right now?" I ask, making sure I have it right. "On the plateau?"

"You seem to be," Dad says. "But there may be a steep flight of stairs just around the corner. And someday, you may very well end up being taller than the boy or girl who's the tallest person in your class right now."

"But *now* is when it's embarrassing, Dad," I say. "Especially because basketball is something I should be naturally good at," I add.

UH-OH. I did not think that last sentence through.

✳ **14** ✳

HERE WE GO

My fancy footwork has failed me.

"You say you should naturally be good at basketball," Dad says, his voice quiet. "And just why is that, son?"

Unfortunately, I am unable to delete what I just said from Dad's mental hard drive, so I have to answer his question. "Because just look at the Lakers and the Clippers," I say, naming Los Angeles's two professional basketball teams. "They have tons of players with brown skin. They really do. So my friends at school must kind of expect *me* to be good at it, too. *I* expect me to be good at it."

And—here we go. My dad is really touchy about skin color, mostly because there aren't that many people with brown skin in Oak Glen, California.

But he should have thought of that before we moved here, shouldn't he?

This is all his fault!

Dad clears his throat. "You are fortunate enough to have many career paths that will be open to you, son," he says, pinning me to the back of my chair with a look. "And certainly not just professional sports. You will finish primary school, and middle school, and high school," he announces. "And then you'll graduate from college. After that, we'll see."

"But I could be playing basketball that whole time, couldn't I?" I ask. "Having *fun*? Getting some exercise?"

"Sure, if you love the sport," Dad says. "But not because of the color of your skin, or because of what people expect you to be good at. And there are other sports as well, EllRay. There's tennis, and golf, and baseball, for example."

"Us kids like *basketball*," I mumble, not meeting his eyes. "B-ball."

"'*We* kids like basketball,'" he corrects me. "You would say, 'We like basketball,' remember. That's the test."

"And I'm okay at the drills," I continue, ignoring the grammar lesson. "So far, anyway. But when it comes time for us to play, I'll be scampering around like a hamster on an exercise wheel while everyone else gets to shoot baskets," I say.

"'Like a hamster,'" Dad repeats, blinking at me from behind his glasses. "That's how you see yourself, son?"

"Not all the time," I say. "Just some of the time."

"Well, here's my advice to you," Dad says, stretching. "Enjoy the game as much as possible, for now. All the ball-tossing, and the coaching, and so on. Squeeze out every drop of fun that you can, while you can. Because there's nothing any of us can do about how tall you will grow, or when—no matter how much we love you."

"I know you love me," I mumble, cringing back into my chair.

Geez. I wasn't asking for *mush.*

"And your mom and I will be on the lookout for some other sports you might enjoy," Dad says. "*With* basketball, not instead of basketball," he adds, before I can object. "It's always good to have a team sport you enjoy and a solo sport, too. One that will last a lifetime."

He sounds pretty sure of himself. "What's your solo sport, Dad?" I ask, watching my foot move the kickball back and forth on the rug.

"Hiking and rock climbing, of course," he says, smiling at me. "Remember the hiking and rock climbing we do on all our camping trips? When we go searching for rocks and fossils for my collection? You're great at both those sports, by the way. Just so you know."

"Thanks," I say, staring down at the ball.

I never thought of hiking and rock climbing as sports before. They're just *fun*.

"Now, turn off that worrying brain, son, and hop into the shower," Dad says. "Wash away those blues."

"Okay," I tell him.

No more Alfie-talk! And no losing my *Die, Creature, Die* privileges for a couple of days, either.

SCORE.

Two points.

And I hop—while the hopping is good.

✻ **15** ✻

PLURALS AND DRIBBLE DRILLS

"All done, spelling champs?" Ms. Sanchez says after Word Challenge, something we do every Monday morning. "Then give the corrected papers back to your neighbors, take a look at your scores, and pass everything forward to me."

Today, our spelling words were all plurals. "Plural" means more than one.

Here is how I see plurals. "Boys" is the plural of boy. "Basketballs" is the plural of basketball. So far, so good. You just add "S."

But plurals can get a whole lot trickier. If there was more than one Joe in your class, there would be two Joes. J-O-E-S. But two *banjos* would end with "J-O-S," not "J-O-E-S."

Luckily, one banjo at a time is usually enough.

Plurals can get confusing with animals, too. Say you have one mouse. If he has a friend, they are "mice," not "mouses." But more than one house is not "hice," it's "houses." It would be fun to say, "*The mice are living in their hice*," but you can't.

By now in life, we are supposed to know most plurals, I think, passing forward my Word Challenge. But basically, you have to *remember* the plural of each word. Because there is no one rule that you can apply to all plurals. That's why I think Ms. Sanchez should call this lesson "memorizing," not "learning plurals."

No offense, English language.

"You may be excused," Ms. Sanchez says when all the Word Challenge papers are on her tidy desk. "But no running, please," she adds, as most of the boys—and some of the girls—jump to their feet.

Because—it is perfect basketball weather outside! Pre-basketball, anyway. The last raindrop fell sometime during "banjos."

And it's finally time for recess!

"Line up for your drills, and take your go-to stance," Coach shouts as we run onto the sparkling playground, still shining from this morning's rain. "Now, now!" he adds, clapping his baseball mitt-sized hands together.

And we line up super-fast. I put my feet a shoulder's length apart, one foot forward, and I bend my knees a little.

"Okay," Coach says. "Running in place on the balls of your feet." He prowls up and down the middle of our two lines. "*Hup, hup, hup!* Who wants to quit running and go eat snackies with the little kids on the teeter-totters?"

"*Me*," Marco murmurs. But I'm the only one who hears him.

You're not supposed to eat on the teeter-totters, as *Mr. Havens* would be the first to tell you. But instead of arguing with *Coach*, we run faster.

I wonder if he is like this with his second grade class? They must be like miniature marines by now!

"Left side, dribble drills," Coach shouts, tossing balls to my line. "Right side, keep running—but in a tight circle this time. Turn those bodies around.

And keep your knees bent. This isn't the Monster Mash, people. Move! Move!"

I start dribbling, and Corey runs like a hundred-battery toy.

"Lower, lower, lower," Coach tells us dribblers. "And now I want you to grab those balls and pivot, still dribbling. Pivoting means that you turn on one foot, keeping it in place. Don't just take off and run, because if you move more than one or two steps without dribbling the ball, that's called traveling. And it's a *bad thing*. Say 'traveling,' everyone. Say it!"

"*Traveling*," the dribblers and the runners all shout.

"Say 'bad thing,'" Coach tells us.

"*Bad thing*."

"Oopsie," Emma cries out, as her bouncing ball skitters away from her like a bank robber trying to make a getaway. Kry snags Emma's ball without missing a beat.

Awesome!

I wait for one of the guys—Jared, Stanley, or Jason, probably—to make fun of Emma for saying

"Oopsie," but no one dares. Not with Coach on the job.

FWE-E-E-ET! Coach's silver whistle blows. "And—come on back and switch sides," he hollers. "No time to lose. *Hup, hup!*"

Coach is tough, but he's fair.

Plurals and dribble drills in the same morning, I think as I run in place, trying to copy Corey's mad skills as I turn in a tight circle. *Run, run, run, run, run!*

"Now for some bounce pass drills," Coach says, grabbing a ball to demonstrate. He bounces the ball toward me once, and I catch it. "Good one, EllRay," Coach says, and I feel like the sun is shining all over me. It doesn't even matter how short I am! "Pass it on," Coach tells me. "Hot potato. And keep those fingertips apart, don't forget."

I bounce the ball toward Marco, who is standing there chewing on his lower lip.

"Catch that rock," Coach shouts at Marco. "Both hands! But don't look at the ball, people. Look where it's *going*. Okay, let's get a few of 'em in the air," he says, tossing a couple more balls into the

mix. "Keep 'em moving, moving, moving!" he says.
"One bounce only. And no ball hogs allowed."

I don't know what a ball hog is, but I can guess.
And I don't want to be one.

"Good job, EllRay," Coach calls out. "You're on

fire, kid! And you too, Kry. Way to go. Now, we're gonna try some swats before we cool down. Ell-Ray," he says, turning to me. "My *man*. Throw the ball to Kevin again. Just a rapid-fire pass this time, no bounce."

And so I shoot the ball straight to Kevin, hoping I am doing the right thing. I keep my eye on Kevin's hands, not on the ball. But before the ball gets to Kevin, Coach's tree-trunk arm appears out of nowhere, and he knocks the ball out of the air—toward Jared, who catches it on the bounce.

"That was a swat. Good one, Jared," Coach says, and Jared's face creases into a rare smile. He looks like a whole new person! "Now, shoot that ball to Emma, Jared. And Corey, you try to intercept it. Then swat it toward Annie Pat."

"No, no. That's okay," Annie Pat says, waving her hands in the air like twin starfish.

Plural, "starfish." Go figure.

"Here it comes, A.P.," Coach tells her. "Heads up!"

And Annie Pat actually catches it.

Nobody is more surprised than she is. She smiles big-time, and her face turns pink.

"And now we're gonna slow it down," Coach tells us. "Just gentle passes, guys. But using *both hands*, and keeping those knees slightly bent. You're like coiled springs, people! Pass those balls toward me. EllRay, I'm putting you in charge of the net bag."

Plural, "net bags." Easy.

I scoop up the net bag and start jamming balls into it. **HUP, HUP!**

"We'll meet again Wednesday morning, during recess," Coach tells us. "Until then, keep handling those basketballs at home. Or those beach balls. Whatever. And if you can, find a wall—*outside*, people!—and do some rapid-fire passing drills on your own. Against the wall, no bounce when you pass. And never stop practicing. Just stand about two feet from the wall, throw *hard*, and work your way back. Got that?"

Not really, I think. But I figure *someone* knows what Coach is talking about. And maybe they can tell me. After all, we have three more recesses before Wednesday morning's coaching session.

"Recesses." The plural of recess. You have to stick that "E" in there, or it would look funny. "*Sss*," like the noise snakes make.

We have this afternoon, tomorrow morning, and tomorrow afternoon.

Coach already said I was "on fire," didn't he? And that's the best thing any grown-up who isn't a relative has ever said to me in my entire life! So who knows how good I'll be by Wednesday morning?

Things can only get better.

Right?

✳ **16** ✳

MR. YEAH BUT

"Hey, EllRay," Marco says, catching up to me as we scuff our way back to class. "Do you like b-ball?"

"Yeah," I say, slowing down a little. "Except no one will ever pass me the ball, I'm so short. Why?" I ask. "Don't you like it?"

"Basketball's too noisy," he says after looking around to make sure no one else can hear. "There's too much yelling and stuff. It gives me a headache *and* a stomachache."

"Really?" I say, trying to imagine it.

I think Marco's problem is that he's a kid who needs a lot of peace and quiet. I guess that's why he likes to play olden days on the grass with his plastic dragons and knights.

But peace and quiet are like endangered species at Oak Glen Primary School.

"Then don't play it," I say, shrugging. "You don't *have* to play, Marco."

"Yeah, but that's being a baby," Marco says. "I'd be eating fruit leather on the teeter-totters before you know it," he says, quoting Coach. "Kids would laugh at me. And anyway," he adds, "I like hanging with everyone—when they're not shouting and stuff, anyway."

He really looks miserable. I have a horrible feeling that he's about to cry.

And crying at school is every boy's worst nightmare.

"Maybe you could wear earplugs," I suggest. "We could make some out of clay."

"Yeah, but then I wouldn't be able to hear it if someone said, 'Heads up!' when they passed me the ball," Marco says. "And I'd still feel like I was gonna hurl."

"Maybe you should try yoga," I say. "That's supposed to make you feel all relaxed, Ms. Sanchez says. Then the noise and stuff wouldn't bother you so much."

"Yeah, but yoga's just for *girls*," Marco says. "At Oak Glen, anyway."

Marco Adair is turning into the type of guy my Dad calls *"Mr. Yeah But."*

"Well, maybe you should ask Coach not to yell so much?" I suggest, starting to run out of ideas.

"Yeah, right," Marco says with a bitter laugh. He shakes his head.

"What about if you ask Ms. Sanchez to ask Coach to play b-ball quieter?" I say as we plod down the shiny hall toward class. We're gonna be late!

"Yeah, but that would be like tattling," Marco says, sounding as if all hope is lost. "Anyway, I don't think she's the boss of him. *But thanks for listening, EllRay,*" he adds in a whisper. Quietly.

"Quietly" and "Shortly." That's Marco and me, I guess.

But—poor Marco!

✳ **17** ✳

FOUL!

At Monday lunch, it is like we have taken a strange but silent vote: *"No b-ball."* Instead, we stuff our faces with food, hang by numb arms and burning hands from the cold overhead ladder, and watch the girls compare fancy Japanese erasers from their collections.

That's a thing, I guess. This week, anyway.

Emma has a panda eraser. Annie Pat's is a tiny dolphin. And Cynthia has a butterfly, which Heather says is the best eraser, because of all the colors. The girls are holding their erasers in the palms of their hands, whispering to them like they are little pets.

Sometimes, girls are just strange. No offense.

I would like to have that dolphin eraser, though. I wouldn't use it, either—even though I am a kid who needs erasers.

Who needs them a *lot*.

But it is now afternoon recess, and basketball is creeping back into our brains. The playground monitor—not Mr. Havens today—is busy keeping little kids from walking in front of moving swings and getting clobbered. So "the coast is clear," as my mom sometimes says.

That means we third-graders can do what we want.

Jared is already practice-dribbling a ball.

"Where's Coach?" Corey asks, looking around.

"Probably in the Teachers' Lounge, with an ice pack on his back. Like Ms. Sanchez said that time," I tell him. But I can't really picture it. Coach looks too strong for that.

"We don't need Coach to play basketball," Jared says, dribbling away.

"Well, we don't need him for practice drills, anyway," Diego says. "But Coach hasn't shown us how to shoot baskets yet."

"*Duh*," Kevin says, making a face at Diego. "You just throw the ball and hope for the best." He crouches and then shoots an imaginary ball, demonstrating. He is probably pretending he is a pro player tossing the winning throw as an invisible crowd cheers.

Marco is playing with his olden days figures on the grass near the picnic table. He's probably just glad no one is yelling. Major is standing next to him, like he can't decide whether to join in Marco's game or grab a kickball and start dribbling.

Annie Pat has wandered over to where we are standing. "I don't know," she says, twirling a red pigtail as she watches Kevin leap around. "I think there's probably an official way to shoot baskets, Kevin. A way you can practice. We should wait for Coach to teach us."

"Be quiet, *girl*," Jared tells her. "Just because you caught the ball *one time* this morning. By accident, probably."

Uh-oh.

Foul!

"Her name is Annie Pat, and you know it," Emma pipes up. She's a little scared of Jared, I think. But for some reason, she always stands up to him anyway.

I start to get the feeling that things are about to go seriously wrong with this afternoon recess. And we have waited for it ever since lunch! But Jared would never dare say something mean to Annie Pat if Coach was around. If he did, Coach would send Jared over to the teeter-totters to eat fruit leather with the little kids. Or make him run laps around the playground.

But Jared's the type of kid who acts up when there are no grown-ups nearby. It's his specialty.

"Ooh, she's gonna tell on Jared. Just like a widdle baby," Stanley jeers, using baby talk as he points at Annie Pat. He wipes his grimy fists in his eyes. "*Wah, wah*," he pretend-cries.

"I'm not going to tell," Annie Pat says, protesting. "I never said I was, either."

"Go play with your stupid eraser, or do some stretchy, bendy yoga," Jared tells her, turning away. "*So lame*," he adds under his breath.

"Yoga's not lame," Annie Pat says.

"Us guys should divide up into teams," Kevin says, after Annie Pat and Emma have joined a nearby group of girls: Kry, Fiona, Heather. They're already laughing together, playing some other game. Tagging and chasing, it looks like.

"Yeah," Stanley chimes in. "Let's divide up, and

then try to get past each other." He rams his shoulder into Marco, demonstrating his bashing skills, I guess.

"I'll choose the first team, because I've got the ball," Jared announces. He really means that he'll be the *boss* of that team. The boss of all of us, if he can pull it off.

Not. Gonna. Happen.

"And I'll choose the other team," Jason says. Like I said before, Jason's kind of chunky. But as I also mentioned before, he always says it's pure muscle, even when nobody asks.

But—*choosing teams!*

I hate it when us guys choose teams, mostly because of how short I am. I'm usually picked last for sports things, never first. Or second. Or even third. I liked it better when we were all on the same team during our training sessions, with Coach as our leader.

But what can I do about this whole choosing-teams thing? Nothing!

I'm not the boss of recess. I'm not the boss of *anything.*

✳ **18** ✳

THE CHOOSING

It is as if a dark cloud has appeared over our section of the playground as the choosing begins. My part of the playground, anyway.

"I choose Kevin and Stanley," Jared shouts.

"Hey! One at a time," Jason objects. "Or else I get to choose Corey and Nate and Marco," he says. "And then I want Major and Diego."

"That's five, loser," Jared tells him.

We aren't allowed to say "loser" at Oak Glen Primary School. But that doesn't mean kids don't say the word. Especially when there are no grown-ups around.

World, meet Jared Matthews.

"Give back a couple of your guys," Jared tells Jason. "Or else you have to take EllRay, too," he says, smirking.

A smirk is a nasty little smile, by the way. My mom told me that once.

But—wait. What? I'm like *last prize* now?

I mean, okay. I'm not super good at basketball—*yet*. I don't deserve any respect. But I'm not bad at it. I'm as good a dribbler as anyone here, aren't I? So far? And didn't Coach give me a shout-out just this morning? That's more than Jared got!

So why pick on me?

"Hey," Corey objects, taking my side. "EllRay's got skills, and you know it."

It's true. I have *small* skills, the kind that kids don't notice.

1. I'm a pretty fast runner, for example.
2. And I'm quick. I learn stuff fast, too.
3. Also, like I said, Coach thinks I'm good at bounce pass drills.
4. And Dad says I'm a good hiker and climber.

But nobody notices the skills I have. They like the big, splashy sports skills.

"I know he can't *dunk*," Jared says, like he just

won a bet. "Just look at him. And scoring is the whole point of b-ball, isn't it?"

"Yeah," Stanley says, piling on. "EllRay would need a ladder or a trampoline to get the ball anywhere near the basket." He looks around for approval of this lame joke, but he doesn't get any.

Everyone's too eager to get started with this bogus game, probably.

"Form two lines, yo," Jared says when he has finished picking his team. He barks out the words like he's trying to copy Coach. "*Hup, hup!*"

"Don't '*hup, hup*' me, ball hog," I mutter.

"Come on, you guys," Jared says to us, starting to get mad. "The buzzer's gonna sound. Two lines! Then I'll start dribbling, and our side will bust through your side while you try to tackle us."

"Dude," Diego says, like he's trying to keep Jared from embarrassing himself. "I think tackling is for football, not basketball. I'm pretty sure it is."

Diego's right, of course. He reads a lot. He knows stuff.

"Fingertips," Jared shouts for absolutely no reason at all. "*Hup, hup!* Charge!"

And his wobbly line of pretend basketball players chugs toward the rest of us. But our side is still just wandering around, wondering what we're gonna do next.

So fair, right?

Over on the grass, Marco has scooped up his plastic figures and is cradling them in the bottom of his T-shirt like it's a kangaroo pouch. I can tell he is looking for a nice, quiet escape to the land of peace and quiet. His face is pale.

"Now! Now!" Jared yells at his so-called team as bodies crash together. He is still doing his Coach impersonation. He is crouched pretty low as he dribbles the ball.

But I'm even *lower* to the ground, of course! And so from out of nowhere, I snag the ball, pivot, and then start dribbling it through Jared's broken line of players—who are mostly busy shoving the guys on my team to the ground. Or trying to.

Jason. Nate. Major.

Corey is a superhero, of course. He is dodging left and right like a pinball, and he makes it through Jared's line. "Over here," he calls to me.

I bounce pass the ball to Corey. He is one of our three best dribblers, remember? And—he catches it!

Away he goes toward the invisible basket.

He would *totally make this shot* if this were a real game.

Corey stops, then spikes the ball in the air like a winner. Which he is.

But—**BZZ-Z-Z!**

Recess is over.

"You guys cheated," Jared bellows over the wriggling pile of players at his feet.

"How did we cheat?" I yell back. "Because we played the game right? Better than you?"

"EllRay and Corey won," Diego shouts, fist-pumping the air. "Yes-s-s!"

"Not for long," Jared mutters as we head back to class. "Payback, dude," he says.

"Payback" means "revenge." In this case, revenge for nothing! But having someone say it to you is like getting handed an extra backpack to lug around for an unknown period of time.

The "why" part of payback doesn't even matter. Once some kid has threatened it, the arguing

is over. It's just a matter or when, where, and how much.

And somehow, I know Jared was talking to me when he said it.

So heads-up, self.

✳ **19** ✳

TAKING ONE FOR THE TEAM

"How did it go with Suzette today? You know, at school?" I ask Alfie later that same afternoon, Monday.

I mean, how did it go at Kreative Learning and Daycare, of course. But lately, Alfie likes us to call it school. I guess she's trying to get used to the idea of kindergarten.

We are curled up at opposite ends of the squashy sofa in our family room. We're eating string cheese and peanut-butter-stuffed celery sticks, our after-school snacks today. Mom is working at her desk.

"It went tewwible," Alfie says, shredding a strip of the white cheese.

"Terrible."

"I had to apologize *twice* about my kindergarten party," she continues.

"Why twice?" I ask. Once would be plenty, believe me—with Suzette Monahan.

"Suzette lied and said she didn't hear me the first time," Alfie explains. "Only now she's getting even."

More payback. Maybe my family is doomed! "How?" I ask. "What's she doing to you now?"

"Having a sleepover. Only I don't get to come," Alfie says, and her chin wobbles a little.

Whoa. My sister is clouding up. Tears fill her eyes.

"But Alf," I say, trying to think of something, quick. "You don't even *like* sleepovers. Remember before Christmas, that sleepover at Arletty's? Dad had to come get you in the middle of the night, you were crying so hard. Mom said you were too young even to have tried it. She said it was a bad idea from the start."

"I only cried because Arletty's dinner tasted weird," Alfie says, defending herself. "They had funny chicken with gween stuff on it. And I cried because Arletty's mom wouldn't leave the light on in the closet when we went to bed. And Mona fweaked."

Freaked. "Dad told us you're the one who was scared," I say, not looking at her.

"*Anyway*, I don't get to go to Suzette's," Alfie says, giving me a look.

"Are you sure it's even a real sleepover?" I ask. "Maybe she's just punking you, Alf. Like you tried to do to her. You know, with that fake party last week."

"It's a sleepover, all wight," she says, nodding her head.

All right.

"And Suzette's gonna get away with it," Alfie continues. "There's nothing I can do."

"But how is that fair?" I ask. "How come you—"

"Because sleepovers are different from other parties," Alfie says, interrupting me. "They *have* to be smaller. You can invite who you want. So I can't even tell on Suzette."

"Would you tell on her if you could?" I ask, curious to know the answer. "So you could get even with her? For getting even with you?"

"Maybe," Alfie admits. "I dunno. I get mixed up about who started things. But I'm pretty sure it was Suzette."

"And anyway," I say, pretending to agree with her, "like you said, it sounds like there's nothing you can do about it. That's the thing."

Just like there's nothing I can do about being too short to dunk a basketball—or maybe shoot any kind of basket. Even a layup, and layups are probably the simplest shot to make. At least I can't do it while I'm still on that moving sidewalk Dad was telling me about. The one where you don't grow on the outside for a while.

I have no way of standing out. Or of standing tall.

"There's *something* I can do about it," Alfie says. "I can be sad all Fwiday night."

"That's when the sleepover is?" I ask.

Alfie nods. "They'll have the best time *ever*, that's all," she adds. "And they'll be talking about it all this week. *Blah-blah-blah*," she says, imitating them in advance.

"And you and I will be here at home, warming the bench on Friday night," I say. I'm trying to let her know she's not alone. She'll have company, at least.

"Warming *what* bench?" Alfie asks, scowling again.

"That's just an expression," I hurry to explain, before her chin starts wobbling again. "*Bench-warmer*. That's somebody who doesn't get to play in the game."

Meet EllRay Jakes.

"Or go to the sleepover," Alfie says. "Suzette's a *bully*, that's all."

I think about it for a second. "I don't know about

that," I finally say. "You and Suzette are sort of the same, Alfie—the same age, and almost the same size. And your fights have always been one-against-one. You guys are even."

"Whose side are you on?" Alfie asks, jumping to her feet so fast that a stalk of peanut-butter-stuffed celery lands sticky-side-down on one of Mom's throw pillows.

"I'm on your side," I tell her. "I'm just saying that you calling Suzette a bully isn't gonna fly, that's all. Not after that trick you played on her last week."

"You're on *her side*," Alfie says, furious. "And you're my brother!"

"I'm not on Suzette's side," I say, hoping to calm her down. "Is Suzette being mean to you, not inviting you to her sleepover? And mean to the other girls she didn't invite? Yeah. Maybe she is. But is there anything you can do about it? Not really, no matter who you tell. It will be over in a few days, though. Sometimes you just have to wait it out."

I feel like I'm coaching Alfie now! *Hup, hup.*

"A few *long* days," Alfie corrects me. "With Suzette going *'ha, ha, ha'* the whole time." She sighs, imagining it.

"Just go '*ha, ha, ha*' right back at her. And then it will be over," I say again.

Alfie's sleepover disaster will be over—just like the whole choosing-teams thing was over when recess ended today. And I'm still short, but us guys can have fun again on Wednesday morning, learning pre-basketball with Coach.

"So I have to be a benchwarmer *all week*, while they get to talk about how much fun they're gonna have?" Alfie asks, trying to get it straight.

"Yep," I say, thinking, So will I, maybe. And for longer than a week. "But you're pretty tough, Alf," I say, trying to encourage her. "And the good thing about being a benchwarmer is that you're still in the game, see," I explain. "You're just waiting for your chance to play. And that time will come."

"And plus, I'll get to sleep at home Fwiday night," Alfie says, her expression brightening. "Not in someone else's scary woom."

Room. "Maybe we can even do something fun on Friday night," I say, hoping to make her feel better. "You and me, Alf. Like play a board game or something."

This is a big sacrifice on my part. With Alfie,

board games usually end with all the pieces flying through the air when she starts to lose.

"Can we play that candy game, or the one with the ladders?" Alfie asks, already excited.

"Sure," I say, hiding my sigh.

I'm taking one for the team, yo.

"Okay," she says, sounding a little happier, at least. "Will you help me clean off this pillow, Ell-Way? Because someone spilled peanut butter all over it."

"Someone did?" I ask, smiling. "Sure. I'll help," I say. "But then I gotta go do my homework, Alf."

It's subtraction word problems tonight. *Woo-hoo.*

"Homework sounds scary," Alfie says, her voice turning small. "Will I have to do homework when I'm in kindergarten?"

"Nuh-uh," I tell her. "Why?" I ask. "Is that what you're worried about?"

"Kinda," Alfie admits. "And not knowing what schools my friends are gonna be going to. So I thought we could start practicing at the party—and be together *now*, at least." Her brown eyes are wide and shiny again with tears that are about to fall.

"Well, I could help out a little," I say, hiding

another sigh—because of course I would rather play *Die, Creature, Die* than teach Alfie how to sharpen pencils and snap the lids on to her markers right. Who wouldn't? "We could play pretend kindergarten," I say.

"Weally?" she asks, blinking.

Really. "Sure," I tell her. "If it would make you feel better about changing schools. Only you can't tell anyone, okay?" I add, thinking of the teasing that might happen at Oak Glen Primary School if word got out that I was playing kindergarten with my little sister.

Alfie presses her lips together until they disappear, and she makes an X across them with a peanut-buttery finger. "*I pwomise,*" she manages to say out of the corner of her mouth.

"It's a deal, then," I say. "We'll start on Friday night, while we're warming that bench."

"Huh?"

"Never mind," I say, standing up—because I have to get started on those subtraction word problems, don't I?

They're not gonna solve themselves!

⚝ **20** ⚝

"BEEF"

"WOO!" I say, slapping Corey's palm in a high-five. We thought Wednesday morning recess—and our pre-basketball session with Coach—would never happen, but now it's here.

Corey's probably a little bit happier about recess than I am, since he's not the one who was threatened with "payback, dude," by Jared the Hulk, or who got made fun of by Stanley for being so short.

But at least it's recess.

"Line up," Coach shouts as we pour onto the playground. Coach is nearer one of the baskets today than he was on Monday. He looks bigger than ever. "Now, now!" he says, tossing us balls as we trot to our places. "Remember your stance, and keep those balls moving," he tells us. "Pivot in *both directions*, too, or else you're just going around in a circle," he adds, making a face. "Remember, you've got two hands and two feet. *Use* 'em."

"When do we get to *play basketball*?" Jared mumble-says, complaining just loud enough for Coach to hear.

"When you're ten," Coach says. "Until then, it's pre-basketball. Pretend you're the sorcerer's apprentice, buddy—and I'm the sorcerer. You'll be ready for the real thing later on—if you keep your eyes and ears open *now*. And *if* you keep practicing."

Jared catches my eye, and of course he passes his embarrassment on to me. "*Payback*," he mouths without making any noise.

Like I've forgotten!

Kry is dribbling away like crazy, with her ball really low to the ground. It keeps bouncing back to her fingertips like there are invisible elastic strings attached. I try to dribble like that, but after a few bounces, Stanley kicks my ball away with a sideswipe move he could never pull off on the soccer field.

Lucky kick—for *him*.

"*Boing, boing, boing,*" he teases quietly, making bouncy trampoline noises.

Because I'm so short, remember?

Oops! Coach saw that sideswipe kick. "Stanley," he says, barking out the name. "One lap. And when Stanley comes back, boys and girls, we're going to try some layups," he tells the rest of us as Stanley goes chugging off.

"Do 'layups' mean we get to take a nap?" I hear Annie Pat ask Emma. She sounds hopeful.

"Probably not," Emma says, panting a little as she tries to keep control of her ball—which seems to have its own idea of where to bounce. It's the opposite of Kry's ball, that's for sure.

1. My pivot and dribble skills are somewhere in between Kry's and Emma's.
2. I'm also worse at pivoting and dribbling than Corey and Kevin.
3. I'm about the same as Major.
4. But I'm a little better than Jason and Jared—and Marco, who is barely even trying today. I'm better than they are in the skills we've learned so far, anyway. Not in size.

It's like there are comparison charts—about *everything*—that are always in my brain.

"*Hup, hup*," Coach says as Stanley comes gasping back to us. "Time for some layups, then we'll have a huddle."

Diego's hand shoots up. "Isn't 'huddle' a football word?" he asks, curious.

"Basketball, too," Coach says. "Okay, layups. They're the most basic shot in basketball, guys. You use *one hand* to shoot the ball, left or right. Like I said before, I want you to use both hands equally well. That could win you the game someday. But you're going to use your right hands today. You'll try to bounce the ball off the backboard, if you can get it up that high. Your goal is for the ball to then go down through the basket. The backboard's your *helper*. And a layup can be a thing of beauty. Watch this," he tells us. "I'll show you."

And Coach heads toward the basket, dribbling his ball all the way perfectly, of course. When he gets there, he jumps off his left foot, and he uses his right hand to toss the ball against the backboard. His hand looks totally relaxed in the air, and his arm stays up there after he's thrown the ball.

WHOOSH!

Bounce-off-the-backboard, basket.

So cool.

"You're using your elbow, forearm, and wrist to shoot," Coach says, dribbling the ball back to us.

"What's a forearm?" Kevin asks Jared, looking worried. "I only got two."

"He means from the elbow down," Diego says, showing him.

"So, now," Coach tells us, "I want you to dribble down the court with your *right hand*, then try to shoot a layup when you get near the basket. We'll try the other hand tomorrow."

Me? *Hit the backboard?*

Throwing the ball the correct way?

Man, I am gonna be so bad at this. I can feel my whole head get hot just thinking about it.

"Don't even worry about making a basket," Coach tells us, like he can read my mind. "You're just getting used to a series of moves. Okay—Jared, Kry, and Corey. Now!"

And off they go, dribbling.

"Right-hand dribbles only, for now," Coach yells. He hollers a reminder. "And jump off your left foot! Shoot with your right arm! Elbows, forearms, and wrists, people. You're not flinging eggs against a wall."

Which sounds like complete and total fun. Let's do that!

"Grab those balls and head on home to me," Coach tells the first three kids. "And get ready—EllRay, Kevin, and Marco. Go! Right-hand dribbles!"

Bounce-bounce-bounce-bounce-bounce-bounce-bounce.

Stop.

Jump left foot, shoot right arm.

And—**PLOOP!** My basketball makes a puny curve through the air, hits the ground, and then goes rolling off on a little field trip of its own. Toward the chain-link fence.

"Good form, EllRay," Coach shouts. And he's not even being sarcastic! "You got it pretty far up there, Kevin," he says to my sometimes-friend. "Too much shoulder, Marco. But good effort, buddy. Now, layups are something you can practice on your own, people—if you manage to snag a ball at recess. But huddle up. There's something I want to tell you before the buzzer sounds. It's '*BEEF*,'" he says as we gather around.

Beef? I'm all for it. Especially hamburgers.

"The letters stand for four words I want you to remember when you try to shoot a basket," Coach explains. "'B' is for *balance*," he begins. "One foot in front of the other."

We shuffle our feet a little, trying it out.

"'E' is for *eyes on the target*. Not eyes on the ball," Coach continues. "Keep that in mind no matter what you do in life."

Okay. *That's* not confusing.

"The second 'E' is for *elbows*," Coach tells us. "Keep them down, right beneath the hand that's going to throw the ball. No flappy chicken wings allowed," he says, demonstrating.

Of course, this sets off a flurry of chicken wing flapping, which Coach ignores.

"And 'F' is for *follow-through*," he says. "You keep that arm *up there* after you throw, like it's still doing its business. You don't waggle your arm around while the ball is still in the air. Let that ball know you care. Commit!"

I care! I care!

But—"*BEEF.*" I'll never remember what those letters stand for, I think, frowning. Not that *and* how to do subtraction word problems, understand negative numbers, and memorize random, goofy plurals.

Not to mention trying to figure out how to watch out for Alfie, so she doesn't turn into the world's tiniest bully again.

And worrying about poor old peace-and-quiet Marco.

And guarding against payback.

My brain is already full, yo.

"Got that?" Coach shouts as the buzzer sounds.

"Got it," we yell back.

And I just hope somebody means it.

Because then maybe they can explain it to me.

✳ **21** ✳

PAYBACK TIME

At afternoon recess, Marco sticks by my side as I rush down the hall toward an exit door. We pass the kindergartner's display of handprints on cutout hearts. I guess they're for Valentine's Day. We pass the fifth- and sixth-graders' combined display for Black History Month.

"What's your hurry?" Marco asks, tugging at my sweatshirt sleeve to slow me down. "Coach probably isn't even gonna be out there, so we can play whatever we want. Something *fun* for a change." He pats his pants pocket in a promising way.

"But I want to play basketball so I can get better," I tell him. "Only I can't even remember what '*BEEF*' stands for."

"I dunno. I wasn't paying attention," Marco says, shrugging as the cool outside air hits our faces. "But are you *sure* you wanna play basketball?" he asks, slowing down even more. "Some of the guys just make up new rules when Coach isn't around, and you know it. It can get crazy out there."

He's right. Remember Jared's football-style charge through the basketball players on Monday? It's like the more rules we learn, the faster we want to throw them all away when Coach isn't with us.

As if it might be our last chance in life just to be goofy kids having fun.

"But listen, *maybe* give basketball a try?" I say to Marco, not looking at him. "I can get hold of a ball, and we can practice. Just you and me. It'll be cool."

"I dunno," Marco says, shrugging. "I'll think about it."

That's usually his way of saying "No."

"You won't even notice the noise and stuff. Not once you start having fun," I say, hoping it's true. "Remember when Coach said, 'Good effort, buddy!' this morning? He was talkin' to you, Marco!"

"I'll think about it," Marco says again. But he's smiling this time.

Hey, maybe I'm coaching Marco *and* Alfie!

"Yo, dog," Diego is saying to Jason as Marco and I get near. Jason is messing around and making funny faces as he dribbles one of the best balls we have—a new basketball. Just looking at it, I can almost feel its promising little bumps. Smell its serious smell.

"Respect," the ball seems to call out to me. *"Being good at a sport. This is how you get there, dude!"*

"I'll give you my snack if you let me have the ball for five minutes. I wanna practice my dribbling," Diego tells Jason. Marco gives me a look, then heads off toward the picnic tables.

I'll catch him later when I snag a ball for us.

"I'm thinkin' about it," Jason tells Diego.

"Can I have the ball after you finish with it?" I ask Diego. "I'm trying to get Marco to start playing more. I think he kind of wants to."

Diego tilts his head, and he gives me a curious look. "You're a good dude, EllRay," he says. "And a good friend, too."

"You *guys*," Jason says. "You gotta get the ball first, don't forget."

"Okay. EllRay will give you *his* snack, too," Diego says, making the deal even sweeter for Jason.

Jason—who is chunky but "mostly muscle," remember—loves food.

You're not supposed to trade snacks at Oak Glen Primary School because of allergies. But nobody in our class is allergic to anything serious—except for Marco being allergic to basketball, I mean. And to noise.

"*Huh*," Jason snort-says, trying to walk in a circle around the ever-bouncing ball the way Coach does. "EllRay probably already ate his snack," Jason says. "And I bet you have something weird, Diego. So thanks, but no thanks. I'll keep the ball."

The afternoon sun shines through Jason's ears from behind, turning them pink.

Diego turns to me. "You really want it?" he asks.

"Yeah," I say. "Like I said, it's for Marco."

Diego thinks fast. "Okay, so no snack," he tells Jason. "But I have money." He pats his front pants pocket. "And money buys *candy*, doesn't it?"

"*Dog,*" I whisper to Diego, tugging at him. "*You're not supposed to bring money to school.*"

"It's for phone calls," Diego tells me, even though that doesn't make much sense. There aren't any pay phones here. Some of us kids have cell phones, even in third grade. But we have to hand them in at the office each morning and pick them up again from Miss Myrna when it's time to leave.

Life gets complicated here at Oak Glen Primary School.

I think maybe Diego just likes having money clank around in his pocket.

"Money?" Jason says, interested. His bouncing slows. "How much you got?"

"Dollar fifty," Diego tells him. "Six quarters, yo."

Geez! That's kind of a lot!

"Here ya go, loser," Jason says after Diego has handed over the silver coins.

We're not allowed to say "loser" at Oak Glen Primary School. That breaks another rule. But by some amazing miracle, the word escapes Jason's mouth anyway.

Go figure.

Diego smiles, then tosses me the ball. "Props to you, dude," he tells me.

"Thanks," I say, surprised.

I take a deep breath and check my stance, moving my weight to the front of my feet, up by my toes. Maybe I'll begin dribbling my way toward Marco. But first I have to get into the rhythm of the thing before someone swats the ball away from me and Diego's money is wasted.

"Hey! EllRay's got the good ball," I hear Jared's boomy voice call out from way across the playground.

"Let's go get it," Stanley shouts back. "Let's go get *him*. Grab Kevin," he yells to Jared.

UH-OH.

Payback time.

22

SWISH SHOT!

I pivot, trying to figure out what to do next, because—are Jared, Stanley, and Kevin gonna just *charge* me? Knock me down like a bowling pin? Pile on and start pounding? All *three* of them? They might get in trouble for it, sure. But I don't think they care, at this point. And there's no one around to stop them.

Diego always says he's a thinker, not a fighter. And we respect that.

But that means *he* won't be much help in this situation.

Corey would try to help me if he was nearby, but he's not. He's even farther away than the three payback guys are. And it's like Corey is made out of pipe cleaners, compared to the way gigantic Jared Matthews is built. Jared is almost like a sixth-grader. Or at least one-and-a-half third-graders.

What is his gripe against me, anyway? Who knows? I can't even remember what happened *this morning*, much less two days ago, when Jared first got mad at me. I just remember his threat to get even.

I keep dribbling the ball the way Coach taught us to, but I gotta go *somewhere!* I can hear six big feet pounding their way toward me.

"Run!" Diego says, like he's reminding me to do some chore I forgot.

"Hey," Corey shouts from way behind Jared, Stanley, and Kevin.

So at least he knows what's going on.

But to turn around and get to Corey, and the chance of safety, I'd have to run all the way across the playground, and then plow through Jared, Stanley, and Kevin—if and when I could get that far.

Me, EllRay Jakes. The smallest kid in Ms. Sanchez's third grade class. With the shortest legs.

And *that's* not gonna happen.

Forget about dribbling the ball, I decide in one quick second. We're not even playing a game, here! This is about *survival*.

So I tuck the basketball under my arm and just start running, like Diego told me to do—toward Marco and the picnic tables. It's like I don't have a choice.

Marco has been digging in his pockets—for some of the plastic figures he has sneaked to school, probably. They always seem to calm him down when kids yell.

Marco "Mr. Yeah But" Adair could probably come up with ten reasons why me racing over to him in the middle of a disaster like this is not a good idea. After all, what is about to happen to me is the exact opposite of the peace and quiet he loves. But I'm doing it anyway.

I have nowhere else to go!

"Marco! Catch," I say, and I throw him the basketball without thinking.

And Marco flings his hands up in the air—more to make me stay away than to catch the ball, I think. A couple of plastic knights go flying.

"Cheater!" an angry voice shouts. It still sounds far away, but it's getting closer.

I think it's Jared.

"Yeah! You didn't dribble, so that was *traveling*," Kevin yells, like we are playing a real basketball game. Not like they're about to gang up on me for no reason.

But Marco already has the ball in his hands. He is staring at it in horror. It's like he is holding a giant tarantula instead of a basketball.

What have I done? I dragged Marco into this—

just when he was thinking about joining in the so-called fun! Now, he'll *never* want to play.

Some coach I turned out to be!

"Just throw it to them, Marco," I manage to say, panting out the words as I reach the picnic table. "Maybe that'll make 'em happy."

It won't, though. They're after *me* now. Not the basketball.

And they're getting closer.

Okay, I gotta say that I am really dreading what will happen next. I can just picture it.

1. Jared will tackle me, and I'll end up face-down on the muddy grass while he grinds his fist into my ribs. I can almost already smell his peanut-buttery breath on my face.
2. Stanley will probably start tickling my armpits. He knows I hate that!
3. And Kevin will just pile on, smooshing me flat.

The point is, this is not gonna be fun.

And on top of everything else, I will have to explain my dirty clothes to Mom—and maybe even

Dad—without tattling on anyone! Because tattling would just start some big *thing* here at Oak Glen Primary School. It has happened before.

Phone calls. Worried parents. Boring meetings. Who knows what.

I'm standing here with my mind racing, but Marco is frozen.

"Oh, give it here," I say to Marco, holding out my hands as I prepare to meet my doom. "It's okay. I got you into this, dog."

"Thanks," Marco says, looking surprised. "You'd do that for me?"

"Sure," I say. He had to ask?

And instead of passing me the ball, Marco aims toward a trash can wa-a-y over by the girls' table. He pauses, and then—**SWISH SHOT!**

A swish shot is when the ball goes right through the hoop without even touching the rim.

In other words, perfection.

"Two points!" I shout, congratulating Marco with a high-five just as Jared, Kevin, and Stanley arrive at the picnic table, red-faced, angry, and out of breath.

"Dude," Stanley screams at Marco. "You threw

our brand-new ball in the *garbage*? With all the cooties from lunch? And the dirty Kleenexes and *girl germs*? There's flies in there, and maybe even bees!"

Stanley has always been scared of bees. When one buzzes into Ms. Sanchez's class, forget about it.

"Let's make him get it out," a scowling Jared says to Stanley and Kevin. "And then let's make him lick it clean!"

"Oh, yeah? You and whose army?" I say, because to my surprise, Corey, Major, Nate, and Diego are here, too.

And nobody's going to be licking *anything* clean.

Marco moves a small step closer to me. I can feel him getting braver by the second—maybe because of this added show of support.

"But EllRay and Marco wrecked our whole recess," Jared tells everyone, forgetting he's the guy who started all this. "They gotta *pay*."

"They're *gonna* pay," Stanley insists, his voice way too loud.

I sneak a look at quiet-loving Marco. Is he about to keel over from all the noise and drama? He *seems* okay. But—"Use your indoors voices," I tell everyone, quoting Mom when she's talking to my noisy sister, Alfie.

Maybe I can still help Marco a little, at least!

"*I'm okay, EllRay,*" Marco whispers to me. "*Really.*"

"Use our indoors voices?" Jared shouts at me, sounding like he can't believe his ears. "But we're *outdoors*!"

"He's got a point, EllRay," Diego says in his common-sense way. "We are outside, you gotta admit."

And I can't help it, I start to laugh. This happens to me sometimes—usually at the worst possible moment.

But Kevin starts to laugh, too. And so do Corey and Nate and Major and Stanley.

Even Marco is smiling. He has started picking up his scattered knights like he's on an Easter egg hunt, but I can see the grin.

Only Jared still wants to drag out the fight. "We can't let them get away with this," he informs his giggling posse. And he actually stamps his foot— like a two-year-old!

I crack up all over again.

"Oh, give it a rest, dog," Nate says to Jared in his usual easy way. "It's over."

"*Well, I'm not getting the ball,*" Jared roars.

And so Marco and I fish the basketball out of the girls' trash can, brushing off banana peels and bologna sandwich crusts—just as the end-of-recess buzzer sounds.

Marco and I are not afraid of bees. Well, not as bad as Stanley, anyway.

And P. S., I tell myself as I walk back to class with Marco, Corey, and the rest of my friends: I don't think recess was wrecked at all. Not when I look at the way Marco is walking. He's feeling *good*.

And I'm standing pretty tall, too!

Recess was **AWESOME.**

✳ **23** ✳

REBOUND

"Suzette is having fun *right now*," Alfie announces in a gloomy voice from her perch on the living room sofa. She likes to part the front curtains an inch or two at night, kneel backward on the center cushion, and "*keep an eye on things*," as Mom puts it.

In other words, spy.

It is a rainy Friday night, and Alfie's correct. Suzette's sleepover is probably going *great*.

Well, that's okay. Alfie can rebound.

"Rebound" means two things, Coach explained that day when he showed us how to do a layup. It means catching the basketball if it misses going into the basket. You get it "on the rebound."

But he said the same word also describes how a *person* can bounce back after something bad happens.

"You know what?" I ask Alfie.

"This better not be a joke," she says without looking at me.

"It's not," I promise her. "I was just gonna say that everything will be over by Monday, and then things can get back to normal with you and Suzette. That's how it works sometimes, being friends with someone," I add, like I'm coaching her again.

"Huh," Alfie says, clearly not convinced.

And then, "He's here!" she shouts, her voice surprisingly loud for someone her size. She flings herself off the sofa, soft black braids bouncing, and Mom's throw pillows go flying.

But who cares? Dad's home!

"I have some surprises for you nice people," Dad tells us after finishing his last bite of mashed potatoes. He takes a sip of ice water in his slow, thoughtful way, then places his barely used napkin on the table.

My own napkin looks like it got into a fight with the gravy jug—and lost.

"Surprises?" Alfie says, sounding suspicious. "They're not surprises that mean we can't watch a movie and cuddle, are they? They're not surprises that mean company is coming over, but they don't have kids?"

"No. It's just us tonight," Dad assures her as I start clearing the table. "First comes Mom, our brilliant chef," he says, getting up from his chair and heading past me toward the back hall.

"Mom always comes first," Alfie half grumbles.

But in my opinion, I think that's the way things should be. Mom is like the queen of our family.

"*Ta-da!*" Dad says, handing Mom her big, soft-looking present. See, Dad told me once that he thinks presents are more fun when they are a total surprise. "Here you go, Louise. I hope you like it."

"Oh, Warren. Thanks," Mom says.

"Ooh," Alfie says, her eyes wide. Mom's present is a beautiful, soft blanket with long fringe, the kind you cover yourself with while you're watching TV. "Can I use it during the movie?" she asks, combing the fringe with her fingers.

"We can share," Mom says, giving my dad a special thank-you look.

"Now me," Alfie says, still holding on to the blanket.

"Here you go, Miss Alfie," Dad says after another trip to the back hall. I wonder what's back there for me?

"Is it breaky?" Alfie asks, taking the gift from him.

That's her word for "breakable." I guess she wants to know how careful she has to be when she opens it.

"Let 'er rip," Dad says, giving her the go-ahead.

And so Alfie tears into the wrapping paper. And out come a purple plastic horse with a long white mane for Alfie to brush, and a lavender baby horse—with wings! Score, Dad.

"Is the baby gonna grow up and be a *unicorn*?" Alfie asks, hardly able to believe her luck.

"Maybe someday," Dad jokes, forgetting how confused she already is about such things.

But I don't say anything, because—*I'm next.*

"A-a-and, EllRay," Dad says after a third trip to the back hall.

My wrapped present is half square and half round, which is confusing. My stomach even gives a disappointed little **BLOOP** for a second, because I was really hoping for a basketball.

"Go ahead and open it, son," Dad says, smiling, as the rain patters harder against the windows. "Get it over with. I think you'll be pleased."

It *is* a brand-new basketball! It's just crammed into half a cardboard box, that's all. I pry it out and give it a welcoming sniff.

It's the real thing, all right.

"Ew, gwoss," Alfie says, glancing up from her two new horses.

Gross.

"He's *smelling* it," Alfie informs everyone.

"Of course he is," Mom says, snuggled under her new blanket. "That's part of the fun sometimes. Like when you smell a brand-new doll's hair."

Alfie thinks about it, then gives the smaller horse a cautious sniff. "It smells pretty," she says. "Just like a unicorn." She starts trotting it across the rug.

Oh, geez. Here we go. Will she *ever* get things right?

"There's a new hoop in the hall, too," Dad murmurs, sidling up to me. *"I just didn't want to get your sister all worked up about you getting bigger presents, that's all."*

"A real basketball hoop?" I whisper back, picturing for a second one of those plastic jobs— even though those are pretty cool when you're in preschool, don't get me wrong.

It's just not what I was hoping for *now.*

But Dad nods. "And Marco's dad is coming over tomorrow to help me set it up. Weather permitting," he adds.

"You could install it halfway up the garage door," Mom suggests, probably thinking I'm worried about being too short ever to make a basket.

"Nuh-uh," I say, shaking my head. "I want it the real height."

"He'll grow into it," Dad tells Mom. "In fact, don't EllRay's pants seem a little smaller to you lately?"

"They're just my regular jeans," I say, hitching them up at the waist. "They still fit fine. Even after three helpings of mashed potatoes."

"I meant their length," Dad says, tilting his head

as I toss my new basketball from hand to hand.

Using my fingertips, Coach.

I stick one leg out for inspection.

There *is* a little more sock showing than usual, come to think of it. Could my pants be shrinking?

"You're growing, son," Dad says, reaching over to give my head a knuckle rub. That's his specialty with me.

"I'm probably not," I tell him, breaking the news.

I mean, I don't want to argue on such a fun family night, but I would know it if I was growing taller. Wouldn't I?

Mom's laugh sounds like falling water. "It doesn't happen all at once, honey-bun," she tells me. "Think how upsetting it would be if it did! You would wake up one morning with your legs hanging over the end of your bed."

Sounds good to me. But I'm afraid to get my hopes up.

"Thanks, Dad," I say, leaning into him as I try to hold the basketball under my arm the way Coach sometimes does.

This is our version of a hug, and I'm going in for it.

✳ **24** ✳

PROUD

"I'm proud of you, son," Dad says quietly after Mom and Alfie have left the room for Alfie's bath. "Marco's father told me how you've been watching out for Marco at school and all."

What? No!

I mean, some things are meant to be private.

But I'm glad my dad is proud of me. That's the same thing as respect, isn't it?

"Marco's okay on his own," I tell Dad.

"I know," Dad says. "But it never hurts to have a friend watching your back. A guy you admire."

"Marco admires me?" I ask, touching the new basketball with my fingertips.

"Don't sound so surprised," Dad says, laughing. "Lots of folks think you're a stand-up guy, EllRay Jakes. I've noticed how much you've been helping your little sister, for instance."

I guess being a stand-up guy is better than a falling-over guy, anyway. Maybe it's even the same thing as being a stand-tall guy!

And coaching Alfie is no big deal.

"Okay," I mumble. "Is Marco coming over, too?" I ask, to change the subject. "Tomorrow, I mean?"

"Of course," Dad says, smiling big. "You guys can hang out together while we dads wrestle with the ladder and the hoop."

"Marco will probably want to play olden days. You know, with his knights and dragons," I warn my dad. "He's kind of stubborn that way. It may take him a while to really like b-ball—even with our excellent new basketball and hoop."

"Marco can be any way he wants to be," Dad says. "And so can you, son. Got that?"

"Got it," I say.

"Then go brush your teeth, and tell your little sister good night," Dad says. "Your mom and I will be in before you know it, to say good night and tuck you in."

I don't really need tucking in anymore, but I'm not gonna say no.

"Okay," I say again. But my jaw is aching from

trying to swallow my yawns. "Come in and say good night anyway, Dad? Even if I'm already asleep?"

I like to know it's going to happen, no matter what.

"It's a deal, son."

"Okay," I say for the third time tonight. "Then good night, Dad."

"Good night, EllRay," Dad says. "And stand tall, son."

I will, too. I've earned the right!

READ *MORE* ELLRAY!

✦ ✦ ✦

EllRay Jakes is NOT a chicken!

"In this lively series launch, EllRay displays **BIG-TIME GUTS** as he stands up to the class bully. Ingenious narration."

—*Publishers Weekly*

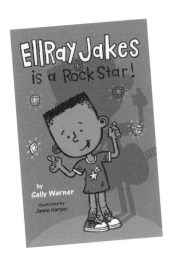

EllRay Jakes is a Rock Star!

"EllRay wants something to brag about [but] his plan for popularity **GOES HAYWIRE**. Kids of all stripes will identify with EllRay."

—*Booklist*

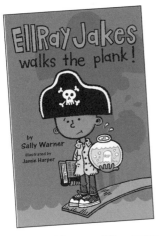

EllRay Jakes
walks the plank!

"EllRay's misguided decision to allow his sister to help take care of the class fish over spring break results in Zip's death, and **TROUBLES CASCADE** from there. The EllRay Jakes stories are just right for his real-life peers." —*Kirkus Reviews*

EllRay Jakes
the Dragon Slayer!

"**ELLRAY JAKES DOESN'T LIKE BULLIES**, so he is naturally very upset when he learns that his little sister is being bossed around by a friend. [Kids] will enjoy reading about EllRay's role as his sister's hero and helper."

—StoryTimeSecrets.blogspot.com

EllRay Jakes
and the Beanstalk

"When his best pal Kevin starts socializing with other kids, EllRay decides to take up skateboarding to impress his former friend. **FAST-PACED** plotting bolsters a narration that feels genuine."

—*Booklist*

EllRay Jakes
is Magic!

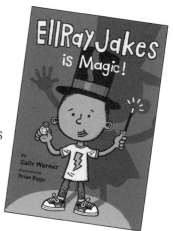

"Eager to avoid performing in the talent show, EllRay and his classmates decide to sabotage the tryouts by only offering up the third grade's worst acts. However, after working to master a few basic 'illusions,' EllRay realizes that maybe he's got a talent worth showing off after all. This contains **SOMETHING FOR EVERYONE**."

—*Booklist*

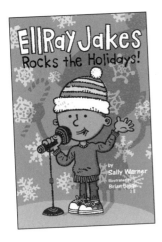

EllRay Jakes
Rocks the Holidays!

"In this **FUNNY YET POIGNANT HOLIDAY TALE**, the African American boy fears that his principal is encouraging him to emcee the school's winter concert merely as a nod to diversity. Another satisfying outing with EllRay."

—*School Library Journal*

EllRay Jakes
the Recess King!

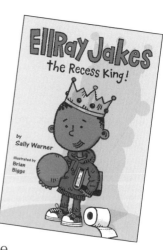

"What's eating EllRay? He's bummed that he doesn't have more friends. This is a simple but **CHARMING** tale, marked by the author's genuine understanding of the elementary school set."

—*School Library Journal*